LOVE DID

BLAKE KARRINGTON

Prologue

"Don't let yourself get attached to anything you are not willing to walk out on in 30 seconds flat if you feel the heat around the corner."

That was my favorite line from the movie *Heat*, a film I had watched easily over a hundred times. Yet, here I stood in need of a reminder of that statement, which had become law in my mind. The crazy thing was, the woman and child who currently had my thoughts going in circles didn't even belong to me. Shit, even worse was she hadn't given me a dime, not one red cent. In fact, *I* had been the one doing all the giving, which was something no other woman could claim.

"Last call for flight number 1705 departing Charlotte, NC, en route to Bali."

Chapter 1

Months earlier . . .

N eville's heart raced as he stood in line at the bank, tapping his foot as he waited to withdraw the money. He kept looking over his shoulder, half-expecting Tomika or her brother to burst through the door. He needed to move and get the hell out of town as quickly as possible.

He tried to focus on putting together the rest of his escape plan. It was rushed, but he knew the first thing was to withdraw all the money he could and disappear before Tomika or her FBI brother could catch up with him.

He racked his brain, trying to figure out where to go as he waited for the line to move, and decided anything down Highway 85 South would work. He had come to this branch because he was typically serviced quickly, but of course, today would be the one day that he needed to rush, and _everyone_ was moving at a snail's pace.

His phone vibrated. It was Tomika calling. He had

blocked her after their confrontation, but it didn't stop her from calling from a private number. Neville pulled his phone out and frowned when he saw "No Caller ID" on the screen. A text popped up. "Your sorry ass is going to jail; I want my fucking money!"

"Excuse me, sir, can I help you?" a voice interrupted his thoughts.

Neville turned to see Regina, the older Black woman who worked as a teller at the bank. She was standing smiling at him as always, and he returned a smile while quickly stuffing his phone into his pocket.

"Hey, pretty lady," Neville cleared his throat. "How are you doing today?"

"I'm doing good, handsome. Just waiting for five o'clock," Regina said, eyeing him. "The better question is, how are *you*?" He looked nervous, and she was concerned.

"Oh, I'm good, luv," Neville assured her. "I just came in because I need to withdraw some funds."

"Okay, well, come on up to my window. You know I'll take care of you," Regina purred flirtatiously.

Neville watched as she swished her hips in front of him, making sure that he paid attention to her curves. Regina was an attractive woman. From what he could tell, she was about ten years his senior and very much single. She wore her hair in a bun. A few stray hairs curled near her forehead. She had very few age lines and skin that looked like she used cocoa butter and Vaseline every day of her life.

"So, how much do you need to withdraw?" Regina asked as she rounded her counter.

"All of it," Neville answered.

Regina paused and gave him another concerned look. "Is everything okay?"

"Oh, yeah, everything with me is great," he lied, looking behind him. "I just need to help my sister. She's about to lose her house."

"Oh, I'm so sorry to hear that. This economy is something else, and these interest rates just keep going up. Now, do you want to transfer the funds or a cash withdrawal?" she asked while her fingers flew over the keyboard and pulled up his information.

"Cash withdrawal, please, beautiful."

"Thank you. Just give me one moment to verify your account."

As Neville watched her work, he felt calm. He knew Regina was attracted to him, and he couldn't help but charm her. He grinned, feeling a little more at ease as he chatted with her. But then he became anxious as he glanced over his shoulder, looking for cops.

"I always feel better when I see you."

Regina blushed and rolled her eyes. "You're such a flirt, Neville. Why aren't you married yet?"

Neville chuckled. "Well, I keep asking you, but you won't say yes."

Regina laughed and shook her head. "You're hopeless."

Neville grinned, but his expression quickly changed when Regina's face turned serious.

"What is it?" Neville asked, feeling a knot form in his stomach.

Regina hesitated, "Uh—well, there seems to be a problem with your accounts. It's not letting me process any withdrawals."

"Why not?" he asked, acting like he had no idea what was going on.

"It looks like they've been flagged for possible fraud," Regina explained as she tapped the keyboards.

"Fraud?" Neville bit his lip. "That's crazy!"

Regina shook her head. "I'm not sure what this is about, but the protocol is to call the police."

Neville tapped the counter. He didn't want to involve Regina in his problems, but he didn't need her calling the law. He looked around, praying he wasn't being set up.

Regina saw the fear in his eyes. Her smile let him know everything was going to be okay. "Don't worry," she whispered. "I don't know what's happening, but whatever it is, it isn't good. When there's a flag like that on your account, it means the cops can freeze your assets for weeks. You need to go, Neville."

Neville nodded, thanked her, then quickly headed out of the bank, keeping his head down until he climbed into the SUV. As he turned to leave, Neville caught a glimpse of himself in the mirror by the door. He looked pale and sweaty, and he knew he needed to get out of town immediately if he wanted to survive.

He couldn't help but replay his last conversation with Tomika in his head.

"Where's my money, Neville?" she demanded, her dark brown eyes blazing with anger.

"I don't know what you're talking about," Neville had replied, trying to sound innocent as he looked at her in the living room of her $750,000 home.

"Don't play dumb with me," Tomika said, stepping closer to him. "I know you took it. You took it all. All these credit cards

you've been opening in my name and the cash advances. It was you! And if you don't give it back to me, I'll make sure you regret it."

That was the last conversation he had with Tomika before he left and blocked her number from calling him.

Neville climbed into his vehicle, gripping the steering wheel as he devised the remainder of his game plan. Luckily, he still had over 10k on him, and he could sell his jewelry to get more if needed. But right now, the most important thing was to get something new popping. So as he merged onto the highway, he reached for his phone and called his connect, Sherri. She was the one that made sure he kept at least three or four CPNs at a time.

"Hello," Sherri answered.

"Hey, it's me, Neville," he greeted, turning down Nipsey Hussle's "Double Up" that was playing in the background.

"Boy, I know who this is. Is everything OK?" she asked with a worried tone in her voice, recognizing that something was off since he wasn't his usual flirty self. He would typically greet her with a "Hey, beautiful" or "What's good, luv?"

"Yeah, everything's good. I just ran into a slight problem and got caught up with this girl, Tomika," Neville explained. "I started messing with her, and things escalated. Finally, she agreed to help me out, making me an authorized user on a few accounts. Then shit went bad, and, of course, she blamed me. Additionally, I just found out her brother is in law enforcement, and now, both are looking for me, and all my fucking accounts are fucking flagged."

"Damn it! What were you thinking, Neville?" Sherri

scolded him. "You know better than to get involved with people with connections like that."

"I know, I know," Neville replied. "I messed up, okay? It's not like I knew the nigga was a cop. But look, I really need your help."

"What do you need?"

"I need all new everything and at least two CPNs already with tradelines on them because it may take me a few weeks to meet someone who can add me as an AU on their accounts."

Sherri sighed. Neville knew it was asking a lot, especially since she knew he wanted CPNs with 800 or better credit scores.

"I'll see what I can do," she said. "But you need to lie low until I get you some new IDs and CPNs. We don't want you getting caught up and blowing up our whole situation."

"I know, I know," he said. "I'm already on the highway headed south, and I ain't stopping until I hit Charlotte. I thought about Atlanta, but there's already too much scamming going on there."

Glancing at the *Welcome to Virginia* sign, Neville just shook his head. D.C. had been good to him, particularly Georgetown, where many highly educated Black women with high-paying government jobs and excellent credit lived. He had his pickings, and they were plentiful . . . until he had to fuck up with meeting the one with an FBI agent for a brother.

Chapter 2

Neville parked his vehicle on the side of the building that had the closest entrance to the room the desk clerk had just given him. Looking up at the extended stay hotel, he silently hoped he wouldn't be there for long. At the moment, he had no access to any of his credit cards, and very few hotels would allow you to check in without keeping one on file. So this weekly hotel was all he could lock in while waiting for a fresh set of CPN numbers and a new ID from his plug. A Credit Privacy Number, or CPN for short, is a nine-digit code formatted like a Social Security number and can be used when applying for homes, cars, etc. He was anxiously waiting on several that had credit scores of 800 and better attached to them. With these CPNs, he could apply for credit cards and anything else that he needed. Until then, this place would have to do.

Neville came from the trenches, and he'd laid his head in much worse places, but this hotel was definitely a far cry from what he'd recently become accustomed to.

He got out of his car and checked his surroundings. He saw a little boy who looked to be about seven years old bouncing a ball in the parking lot. Standing near the hotel entrance, he didn't see any adults around. The boy lost his hold of his ball, and it rolled toward Neville, who stopped it with his foot. He leaned down, picked up the ball, and extended it toward the brown-skinned little boy with a missing front tooth and sandy-brown hair.

"Here you go, Li'l Man. You got to work on them handles."

The child looked up, smiling. "Thank you, sir."

"So, who's your favorite player?"

"I like Kyrie. Who you lik—"

"Assad!"

Neville looked up and saw a frantic woman rushing toward them. The first thing he noticed was her look of fear and worry. She had the same sandy-brown hair as the boy, but her skin tone was just a tad bit lighter. She stood around five foot four, with a plain yet attractive look. Her jeans hugged her curves, and her tight work shirt accentuated her petite figure.

"Assad, what have I told you about talking to strangers?" she asked the child wearily before turning to Neville and giving him a once-over.

"He was standing by the door. His ball rolled over here, and I handed it to him. He didn't say anything to me besides thank you," Neville explained to her in a friendly tone.

The woman nodded and let out a gasp of air. "Thank you for getting his ball for him. Come on, Assad. Let's go," she spoke in an exasperated tone.

"Assad. That's a nice name."

"Thank you," the woman stated slowly as she narrowed her eyes at Neville, and he smiled and laughed lightly while holding his hands up.

"I swear to God I'm not a weirdo. I was just complimenting the li'l man on his handles. You don't have to watch out for me. Trust I'm not on no creep shit. I'm only here because I hit a tight spot and am waiting for something to come through. Hopefully, it's just for a few days until my living arrangements are secured. I'm right here in room 241. What about you? How long have you been staying out here?"

"Yeah, we've been here for nearly two months. I-I hit a bit of a rough patch myself." She shifted her weight from one foot to the other and then continued. "I'm currently on the waiting list for some apartments right now. I really hope it comes through soon because although it's okay, this is nowhere I want to be long-term."

Neville nodded. "I understand that. By the way, I'm Neville."

"Hey, Neville, I'm Lauren."

"OK, Lauren, I know I've taken up enough of your and Li'l Man's time. Hopefully, I'll see y'all around." He nodded his head at Assad, and the boy smiled.

Neville watched as she walked away. She definitely had a nice body under those clothes, but no matter how cute she was, she was staying at this hotel, which meant she didn't have much. And a woman that didn't have much couldn't do much for him. He was already in a bind, so he didn't need a woman who needed help. Instead, he needed one that could help him.

Even though most of the CPNs would come with high scores, he always got extra ones that didn't have tradelines, so he would need someone to add him and those numbers to their credit lines as an authorized user. That's where his charm and great looks came into play. Neville would fuck them delirious and finessed them to add him to their accounts. He'd learned of his gift at the tender age of eighteen when older women used to fall all over him. He had ladies twice his age damn near begging for the dick, and when he served it up, they fell in love. Anything he desired was often given to him by the classy, financially stable older women he was sexing.

As he got older, he took it to the next level, knowing he couldn't just depend on what they would give him. So Neville stepped it up when he got into credit and home loan hustles. He would get credit cards with extremely high limits and make cash advances with most of the balance. The rest he'd purchased top-of-the-line furniture, jewelry, clothes, and shoes. Sometimes, he would return them all for cash or credit back to his debit card. But his new and latest hustle was home title fraud. In fact, that was why he was presently on the run. He had gotten nearly three hundred thousand on a second mortgage on the home of his last victim. Problem was, Tomika never told him that her brother was an FBI agent, and by the time she said it out of anger, he already had the loan approval and wasn't turning down that money. Her timing and his greed had resulted in all of Neville's accounts being frozen.

Now, here he was with no access to all that cash and stuck at this rundown hotel. All he could do was shake his head as he approached his room.

He opened the door and looked around. It looked clean enough, and it didn't smell too bad. That's about all he could ask for. Neville sighed and sat down on the couch in the room. They never lied when they said all good things come to an end. He had been doing his dirt for years, and he almost felt invincible . . . until this shit with Tomika. She seemed to be the perfect mark since she was a nurse and had her life together for real. Having only one child and a good baby daddy that got the daughter every other weekend and paid a hefty amount in child support, Tomika was the type that liked to hustle and get to a bag. So when the hospital had a shortage of RNs, she took advantage and racked up overtime for weeks. She was clocking sixty-hour workweeks like it was nothing, and her paychecks were hefty.

Because of her hustler mentality, she had outstanding credit, a nice four-bedroom home in the suburbs, a Range Rover, and a substantial savings account. However, she was smarter than most, and it wasn't easy for Neville to get her to give him money. So instead, he convinced her to make him an authorized user on a few of her accounts to help him build his credit. Once he got her personal information, he used it with a friend who worked at Wells Fargo to get a line of credit against her home. By the time she found out, he had maxed out the credit line. The only issue was Tomika's brother being a fuck Fed, and neither of them would rest until Neville's black ass was in prison.

His charming good looks and nice, full beard couldn't get him out of this situation. His cognac-colored skin and curly black hair made him a hot commodity among the ladies. Neville didn't work, so he had the time to be a gym rat, and he had a tattooed body that made women drool. He rarely heard the word "no," and he was innovative enough to con his way into anything he wanted. Unfortunately, now, the FBI was on his trail, and he had to lie low, but he couldn't lie all the way low. Neville had to get back in the game and get some money in his hands.

The Feds had frozen all his accounts and any cards linked to the CPN numbers they busted him using. The friend at the bank had broken down quickly and gave up the whole scheme and information they didn't even ask for, including all his other numbers and accounts. Neville always kept cash for emergencies, so he had about $14,000 when everything went down.

He knew that money wouldn't last long after covering the hotel, food, gas, etc., but he couldn't get to some new money or lock another place down until he had some fresh numbers and a new identity. One good thing about coming from the bottom was that there was nothing for him to start over. He didn't care about leaving behind thousands of dollars' worth of furniture or abandoning the spacious town house he was renting. Besides, he hadn't broken a sweat to earn any of the bread he used to acquire his material possessions.

Shit, Neville already had an idea of where he wanted to live next. He just needed those numbers to come through and fast. Anything that he lost, he would replace double.

"Assad, the next time you walk away from me, you are going to get in big trouble," Lauren told her son as they walked away from Neville.

She didn't think the man had been up to no good, but people were weird, and kidnapping and sex trafficking were real. After working a ten-hour shift, the last thing

Lauren needed was to come home to a child that didn't listen.

"But you were taking too long," her son whined, and through her exhausted state, Lauren had to remind herself to be patient.

"I was paying for the room so we can have a place to live next week. I don't care how long I take. If I tell you to stay put, that's what you do," she chastised her son. "Now, get ready to eat dinner, so you can shower and go to bed." Lauren was weary and felt she would break soon if something didn't give.

She had to close her eyes and count to ten in her head when Assad groaned. "But I don't want to go to bed."

It took everything in her not to turn around and walk right back outside. She needed some fresh air and a break. She loved her son with everything in her, but some days, Assad could be a lot—especially when she was in a bad headspace due to her shitty life. She placed two slices of pepperoni pizza in front of her son.

"Eat," she told him in a soft tone.

Assad pouted as he picked up the pizza, and Lauren stared out the window. She kept waiting for life to get better. The only thing she liked about her job as a waitress was that she didn't have to wait a week or two for her paycheck. She could wake up broke, go to work, and come home with $200 in her pocket. Some days were better, of course, and Fridays were always busy, which was why she elected to work a ten-hour shift. Saturdays were good, but she couldn't always work on the weekends when Assad didn't have school.

The only people she trusted to look after him were Aunt Mary and Cousin Felicia. However, she didn't like to burden them either, so if one of them watched him Saturday, she'd get the other to watch him Sunday, and then she'd take the next weekend off.

Last weekend when she worked Friday, Saturday, and Sunday, she made $900. Then she had to miss the next four days because Assad was sick and couldn't attend school. It was as if she took two steps forward and got knocked back four.

One too many slow days at work the month before had been why she fell behind on her rent when her car had to be put in the shop. Spending $600 to get it fixed *and* paying rent wasn't possible. Catching the bus was too hectic and had her late one too many times, and she couldn't afford Ubers, so she got her car fixed—which put her behind, and once she fell into that black hole, she couldn't get herself out. She got evicted, and with an eviction on her credit, no one else would rent to her other than the low-income housing people, and that waiting list was as long as hell. Lauren knew people on it for six-plus months, and she prayed that wasn't the case with her. Like she told Neville, the hotel was better than being homeless.

Her mother was in prison for drugs and theft, and her father was dead. Her aunt lived in low-income housing, and no one was allowed to move in with her. Plus, she only had a one-bedroom anyway. If Lauren really needed it, she and Assad could have slept on her aunt's couch for one or two nights, but they couldn't move in. Her aunt wasn't going to risk being evicted for them. And Felicia had four kids, and they lived in a two-bedroom.

Assad's father was murdered during a drug deal when Assad was three, so Lauren was alone, except for her best friend, Lakesha. Lakesha worked at a bank, so she wasn't rich, but her boyfriend was a dope boy, and when he blessed her with cash, she would buy Assad clothes and shoes, take Lauren grocery shopping, or go out for dinner and drinks. Lakesha's generosity and kind words kept Lauren from having a meltdown. She often volunteered to keep Assad. Lauren just didn't like to bother her on the weekends because her boyfriend was always taking her out of town or wanting to take her out on dates, and Lauren didn't want to interfere with that. She was glad someone was out here living her best life because she didn't know what that was.

As Assad ate his pizza, Lauren eased over to the kitchen area and pulled a cheap bottle of wine from the mini-fridge. After she got a money order to pay for the room for another week, she had enough money for pizza, $10 worth of gas, and a bottle of wine. Since the room was paid for, she hoped she could leave work tomorrow with at least $200. Tomorrow was also food stamp day; after work, she'd shop for the two of them. Lauren got tired of being depressed, so she tried to find something to look forward to each day, but that was becoming harder to do.

Chapter 3

L auren hummed to herself as she did her laundry. It had been a pretty good day. It was a Saturday that she could work, and Lakesha had volunteered to keep Assad. She had gone to work and was able to leave with $215 in tips. After work, she went to the grocery store. There was only so much space in the mini-fridge of the hotel, so she couldn't buy tons of meat and perishable items. So instead, she went shopping for snacks, light food, and beverages for Assad and her, and the room was now stocked up.

By the time she finished, Lakesha and Assad were still at a birthday party, so she cracked open her wine, cooked a quick meal, then headed down to do some laundry. Even though she had worked and come home to do chores, the small break from her son allowed her to relax. She was happy she had somewhere to stay for the next seven days, plenty of food, and a little money in her pocket. Lauren hoped Sunday would be good for her too because she was off Monday and Tuesday. She'd work seven days a week if it were up to her. On Thursday, Aunt Mary would watch Assad after school so that she could work another ten-hour shift.

Neville entered the laundry room with his fine ass. She hadn't seen a man as handsome as him in a long time. Cute men came into the restaurant all the time, but none of them had ever made her stop and stare the way he had. His whole swagger and aura were one of confidence without conceit, which intrigued her. Once she was some-what comfortable that he wasn't a creep, she got lost in his eyes, and his good looks had her vagina feeling things she hadn't felt in a long time.

"Hey. Lauren, right?" he asked as he placed a small duffel bag on the counter and pulled change from his pocket.

"Yes," she replied with a smile.

"Where is Li'l Man?"

"He's with a friend of mine at a birthday party. He should be coming back very soon." Despite knowing that Assad may be back soon, Lauren felt the sudden urge to fold her clothes slower just to remain in Neville's presence.

"That's what's up. I'm glad Li'l Man is out having fun." Neville kept to himself, but every time he saw Assad out playing over the last week, he was alone and looked lonely.

"Yeah. Me too."

Silence loomed. His comment had been simple enough. She knew he'd meant no harm, but it made Lauren sad. There were too many times she wanted to take her son to places like Chuck E. Cheese and let him play until his heart was content, but they'd have to settle for the park because it was free. She had to work an extra few hours just to be able to take him to luxuries like the movies. Even going to the matinee wasn't cheap because Assad would always cry for popcorn and a drink, and Lauren felt if she had to deprive him of something as simple as popcorn and a soda, she shouldn't even take him in the first place.

Neville sensed the shift in her mood. He didn't want to be presumptuous, but he could tell she had the weight of the world on her shoulders, trying to provide for herself and Assad. This hotel was surely not the place to raise a child. Most people living there were truckers or people who had fallen on hard times. And there were rarely times that parents went through hardships that the children didn't suffer right along with them. Neville had experienced this firsthand with his own mother. He watched her work herself into an early grave trying to take care of both of them while supporting her drug habit. This was something he had tried to remove from the depths of his mind and heart, but it was still buried deep down inside. He now felt an immediate urge to show some kindness toward her and the little boy. However, he didn't want to offend her by offering her money and telling her to treat her son. He didn't know them well enough for that not to come off looking crazy.

While both tried to decide what to say, the bell over the door chimed again. They both looked toward the door, and Lauren saw a drop-dead gorgeous woman coming through the entrance. She stood around five-seven, with flawless ebony skin and curves for days. Her long, curly hair hung down to the middle of her back, and she was dressed in designers that Lauren could barely pronounce. The aroma of expensive perfume filled the air of the laundromat, and her diamond-studded earrings gleamed under the lights.

She was bad for sure, and Lauren watched as she headed directly for Neville. Lauren's eyes went to the window and saw a red Mercedes-Benz parked beside Neville's Porsche. So, this was the kind of woman that he liked? The woman sauntered over to Neville with a seductive grin on her face.

"Why are you in here?" She looked around with a scowl on her face. Simone briefly watched Lauren fold her clothes. The woman was pretty enough, but she wasn't anything to do a double take at, so her slight jealousy evaporated. The woman's bushy ponytail could use some heat to straighten it out, and she needed to slap some edge control on those frizzy edges. Her nails were short and didn't even have a coat of clear polish. She didn't even have a gloss on her lips. She was as plain as the day was long. Simone's attention went back to Neville.

"I told you I would do your laundry for you."

"I know you did, and I told you I'm a grown man that can do his own laundry," Neville replied flirtatiously. Simone was a boss. She had created several journals for women, had a candle line, and consulted with other business owners to help get their businesses off the ground or to help them generate more sales. In addition, she offered courses and eBooks, and her considerable social media following allowed her to sell out anytime she had anything to offer. Her last business course was priced at $175, and she had more than one hundred people enroll. Her personal and business credit were A-1, and Neville planned to get what he could from her. He had met a married woman the night before. She was an orthodontist, and her husband was a lawyer. Neville's new list was growing by the day, and he was ready to get back to the hustle.

At first, Neville hesitated to let her know he was staying at the extended stay because a man of his caliber usually only did five-star hotels. One of the reasons he could get women with money was because he looked and played the part. They were more willing to help him when they thought he had his own money. He never came across as a bum nigga. That's not how he got down.

"I just want you to know I have your back," Simone pouted. "Any luck with finding a place?" She was under the impression that he had been a victim of identity theft and his lease had ended before he could decide on a new place, and now he was forced to wait until his new cards and information came, which was half true.

"I went and looked at two places today and narrowed it down to one. I will talk with the leasing office Monday and see if I can start the process."

"That's good. So, are you coming over tonight?" Simone pushed her body into his, and Lauren tossed the last of Assad's clothes into the basket and made her way toward the exit. She didn't care to hear Neville's answer.

As she walked toward the door, Lauren wasn't sure why she felt the sting of jealousy. She didn't even know this man. Yet, she was jealous, though. She wasn't sure if she was jealous that the woman in Neville's place would get filled up with his dick. Or was it that there were women out here with their shit together while she was nowhere near having life figured out. Lauren hated it for herself, and she hated it for Assad. One day, she told herself. One day, she would have her shit together.

FOUR DAYS LATER, LAUREN SAT OUTSIDE THE HOTEL room inside her car with her face in her hands. It was one of the days that she was overwhelmed and tired. When she dropped Assad off, the teacher handed her a slip of paper with the details of a field trip that the children would be taking in three weeks, and the cost of the trip was $55. On top of that, when he was getting dressed for school that morning, it took him too long to put on a pair of his sneakers, and she discovered he'd outgrown the shoes. All his shoes were the same size, so if he couldn't wear those, she was sure he couldn't wear the others.

She'd also called the office of the low-income housing she was waiting to hear back from and was told there were four people on the list ahead of her. At the extended stay, she didn't have to pay a light bill, water bill, or cable and internet bill, but the cost to stay there monthly was almost $500 more than what her rent would be in income-based housing. That was money that she could be keeping in her pocket. The place wasn't even a top-tier hotel, and it was way too expensive to stay there long-term, but it was that or be homeless.

Lauren knew she could call Lakesha and ask her to buy Assad some shoes, but she was tired of having to do that shit. The fact that it was so hard for her to provide the bare necessities for her son made her feel like a failure.

Lauren jumped at the sound of someone knocking on her window. Her heart raced as she looked up and saw Neville. Embarrassed, she wiped the tears from her face and rolled down the window.

"You okay, luv?" he asked with a face full of concern.

Lauren was caught red-handed, so she wasn't sure how to lie.

"Yes, I'm okay. Thank you for asking. It's just one of those days a girl goes through," she tried to laugh, but Neville could see in her eyes that she wasn't okay.

"Can I get in?" he nodded toward the passenger seat.

"Um, sure," Lauren replied nervously. She still didn't know him. All she knew was that he was handsome, dressed nicely, smelled good, and drove a nice car. But on the other hand, maybe he was a pimp and was about to try to recruit her ass.

She watched as Neville walked around to the passenger side of her car and got in. He looked over at her, and Lauren felt herself becoming aroused. She forgot all about being sad because the smell of his cologne was so intoxicating. His stare was turning her on, and maybe what she needed to get her mind off her troubles was some dick. But she doubted she was his type judging from the kind of woman he seemed to go for.

"Talk to me and tell me what's up. I know you don't really know a nigga, but how did you get here? What's your story? Don't tell me you're okay and nothing is wrong because I can see you're going through some shit."

Lauren hated feeling like a charity case. The way he was gazing at her so sympathetically almost made her feel pathetic. But the sincerity in his tone made her want to pour her heart out to him. What was the use of pretending? A blind man could see that she didn't have shit.

"Assad's father was killed a few years back. He wasn't rich, but he helped me out, and I made decent money working in a warehouse. He didn't work a traditional job, so he was able to babysit while I worked, and it worked for us. Unfortunately, when he got killed, my entire life began to crumble. I was so depressed that I lost my job, but thank God, income tax season was right around the corner, and I used that money to pay my rent for a few months and to stay afloat.

"I got a day care voucher and put Assad in day care. I had my months. Some months I struggled, some months were okay, but we were making it . . . until Assad got the flu, and I missed four days of work. Day number three put me on my third strike, and day number four was when I got fired.

"I was only out of work for a month before I found another job, but things were still behind, and I was sinking deeper and deeper into this hole that was becoming harder and harder to get out of, and now I just feel like I'm fucking drowning."

"Damn," Neville chimed in.

"For a long time, I hung on by a thread. Each year at income tax time, I'd have a little cushion to pull myself out of a hole, but an unexpected car repair or something always came along to put me right back at square one. I recently got evicted from my place, and I don't have a lot of family and friends, so I need to stay here if I don't want to sleep in my car. There are cheaper hotels, but I can't have Assad living among pimps, prostitutes, and drug addicts. I've failed him enough," she added sadly.

With how he lied and played games, Neville wasn't sure he had a heart, but Lauren's story tugged at his heart-strings.

"Yo, don't say that. You haven't failed Li'l Man. In fact, you have done a wonderful job with him. He is so polite and well behaved. Take it from a man raised by a mother in similar circumstances, y'all are superwomen to us. We all go through things, luv. What you're going through is fucked up, and I hate that for you and Assad. But I can tell you are one helluva mother with an awesome son."

Lauren offered Neville a small smile. "That he is, but not sure about me, though. This shit gets hard sometimes, but I'd do anything for that little boy. That's why it bothers me so much that I can't do everything I want to for him. For example, I had to send my son to school today with shoes too little for his feet." The moment the words left her mouth, Lauren broke down once again. She felt like a complete and utter failure.

Neville watched her cry, and he didn't know what to do. After a few moments, he reached into his pocket and counted some bills. He got word from his connect that his ID and CPN numbers would be ready in two days. As soon as they came in, he would look for a place to live and get back on his grind. He could afford to look out for Lauren a little bit, which was pretty foreign to Neville. Since he only dated women with money, the most he had to do was wine and dine them for two dates, no more than three. By the time he treated them like queens for a bit and sexed them crazy, he always had them eating out of the palm of his hand, and it would be *their* turn to treat him. Neville *always* got way more than what they gave him willingly . . . or unwillingly.

"Lauren, this isn't much, but it's $500. Get Assad some shoes and whatever else he may need."

Lauren sniffed and looked down at the money in Neville's hand. No matter how much she needed it, she didn't want to owe him anything. She barely knew this man, and he was offering her $500? He'd for sure come back at some unexpected time demanding sex or some-thing crazy, and Lauren wasn't up for it. Granted, she wouldn't mind having sex with him because he was so damn fine, but if she did have sex, it would be on her own terms. She'd never sold her body before and didn't want to start now.

"Oh, um, th-thank you. I appreciate the offer, but I can't pay you back, and with all due respect, I don't want to owe you anything. I really appreciate your offering, though."

Neville smiled. "There is no catch. You don't owe me anything. I put that on my dead mother. I just want to see that little boy happy, and he can't be that if you're not happy. I'm just a humble man who's in a position to do something for someone else. That's it. Where I'm from, $500 isn't a lot. It's not like I'd feel like I own you for giving you this small amount of money."

Lauren shook her head and smiled. She wished she was at the point in life where she viewed $500 as "not a lot of money," but at the moment, it would save her life. However, she still hesitated to take the money from Neville, and he extended his hand farther.

"Lauren, you don't owe me anything," he repeated.

Finally, she took the money. She hated that she had to, but she couldn't let pride stop her from receiving the blessing she needed. "Thank you so much, Neville. I'm going to the mall right now and getting Assad some shoes."

"Get yourself and him whatever you need." Neville reached inside his pocket and pulled out $200 more. "In fact, get your hair or nails done. Treat yourself." He eyed the denim jeans, black fitted shirt, and black flip-flops she wore. Lauren was super plain every time he saw her, and she was still so pretty. He knew if she fixed herself up, she'd be bad as fuck.

Lauren smiled at him bashfully. Did she look that bad? "Thank you," she replied in a low voice, and Neville got out of the car.

Lauren wasted no time going to the mall and shopping for deals. She was in no position to spend half the money she was given on shoes for a six-year-old. She wanted the shoes to fit him and be nice, but she wouldn't go broke in the mall trying to get him shoes to keep up with other kids. She told herself that maybe by the time the weather changed, she'd have the money to get him some Timberland boots. For now, she settled on two pairs of Nikes that were on sale for $60 each. She was so happy to have the money from Neville that she went to TJ Maxx next and got Assad four new outfits to go with his shoes. When she picked him up from school, she would surprise him with a happy meal from McDonald's and ice cream.

Lauren also made an appointment for the next day to get a blowout, and she wasn't going to waste any more of the money. So rather than getting her nails done, she got some press-on nails, and she would do her nails herself. When she stopped and filled her gas tank, it was time to get Assad from school. What had started out as a terrible day had turned out to be great, and she had Neville to thank for that.

Chapter 4

"Oh my God, Neville, I'm about to come!" Simone screeched as Neville pounded into her from behind.

Low grunts escaped his throat as he fucked her hard and fast. Neville gripped her waist and tried to fuck Simone into a coma. Her body smacked into his forcefully as she fucked him back, and he could tell her orgasm was near because she went from running from the dick to sexing him like a possessed woman.

"That's what I'm talking about. Throw that ass back." He smacked her hard on her left cheek. In fact, he slapped her so hard it left a handprint on her round behind. Neville liked rough sex, and Simone did too. They were sexually compatible, which would make his time with her fun.

"Neville, baby, shit!" Simone screamed as she came. Neville grunted and groaned as her vagina gripped his tool like a vice. He was on the verge of an orgasm himself, so he kept his strokes at the same pace.

"Baby, I want you to come all over my face," Simone moaned like the true freak that she was. Neville snatched his dick out of her, pulled off the condom, and began to stroke his dick over her face. She stuck her tongue out seductively and squeezed her breasts in her hands as Neville came all over her pretty face.

While she went into the bathroom to clean up, he started putting together the words and scenarios he would use to ask her to add him to a few of her accounts as an authorized user. Simone had plenty of business and personal credit cards that he knew would send up the scores of the CPNs that were blank.

"That was so good," she grinned as she came out of the bathroom.

"I'm going to sleep like a baby tonight. I wish you were sleeping with me." She wrapped her arms around his waist.

"You know I would love to, but this shit with my credit really has a nigga's mind racing. I spoke with the credit bureau earlier, and although they will clear my account of the fraud, it means my credit will be clean with no prior account information. So it's like I'm starting all the way over from scratch, and I need my score to be up to move into my new place."

"Baby, don't be stressing about that. I told you I'm here for you. I can add you to mine. I have plenty of accounts."

"Damn, you would do that for me, babe?"

"I sure will. Now, can you lie back down and let me see how it feels to wake up with you beside me?"

"I think I can arrange that." Neville would do whatever he had to do to make Simone happy tonight.

CEDRIC SAT AT HIS DESK, STARING OFF INTO SPACE. AS an FBI agent, he always stayed stressed. His job came with nothing but headaches, but this case he was working was pissing him off because he couldn't get a lock on Neville's ass. The condo that he was living in was now vacant. There were no other known addresses for him, and just like that, his ass was a ghost. All his accounts and debit and credit cards had been frozen. It was a lot of money that he now didn't have access to, but he was somewhere hiding out.

The fact that Neville had ruined his sister's credit and taken money from her bank account had Cedric livid. Neville wasn't a completely heartless monster because he'd at least left Tomica with something. Still, the money she had left was nowhere near the five figures she possessed before Neville accessed her computer and got into her bank account. He was a low-life piece of shit, and Cedric wanted to beat Neville's ass before throwing him under the jail. The fact that his weak ass went around preying on hardworking women made Cedric sick to his stomach.

A knock at his door brought him out of the daze that he was in. "Come in," he bellowed before looking down at the file that he had created on Neville.

Agent Don Ramirez knocked lightly before entering Cedric's office, eating a donut. "Any new leads on that case you're working on?"

"Not one. The son of a bitch was smart enough to move out of the condo that he was living in. Nothing that he has is in his name. He obtains cars, places to live, and even bank accounts under false identities. The bank accounts that we had frozen weren't even under his real name, and because of that, I have no way of knowing where the hell he is. The bastard has probably moved onto another name by now and his next victim," Cedric stated with disgust as Ramirez sat down.

"We'll get him. One thing about greed is it will get you fucked every time. He's out there using new CPN numbers, and it will only be a matter of time before he slips up. Just stay on his ass."

Cedric appreciated the words of encouragement. Seeing his sister break down and cry after this man basically robbed her blind and ruined her life was something that he would never forget. He would stay on Neville's ass until he had paid for the hurt he caused.

One thing he had to give to Neville was that he wasn't stupid. One of the bank accounts that had been frozen was in the name of a person that had been deceased since 2018. Neville had opened up major credit cards in the man's name, with more than $30,000 in one bank account. He thought Neville would surely try to grab that money, but he still hadn't.

Cedric also ran the name to see if Neville's car was under that name, but it wasn't. They had, of course, frozen the cards he had obtained using Tomica's information. She had been trying to buy a house when she found out just how badly Neville had messed up her credit. As a result, she couldn't get the dream home she had worked so hard for, and Neville had to pay for that. His sister was still trying to put the pieces of her life back together, and she hated the day that she met Neville's ass. He was the ultimate fuck boy, and she hoped he got what was coming to him.

Chapter 5

L akesha smiled at her friend as Lauren sipped from her glass of wine.

"Okay, I see you with your fresh blowout and those cute-ass nails. I haven't seen you wearing your hair any other way but in a ponytail for damn near a year. What's going on with you? You got some dick?" she asked, waiting for the tea.

Lauren giggled. She wished like hell that she'd gotten some dick, but instead, she said, "No, I haven't gotten any, but that would be the icing on the cake. I met this guy, but it's not like that."

Lakesha looked confused. "What do you mean you 'met a guy, but it's not like that'? Where did you meet him?"

"He's staying at the same extended stay hotel as me and Assad."

Lakesha frowned up her face, but she quickly caught herself because she didn't want to offend her friend, but Lauren had already seen the look.

"He drives a Porsche truck, and he dresses really nice. He's handsome as hell, and I overheard him telling someone he was about to get a place. His stay there was just temporary."

Again, Lakesha didn't want to offend her friend, so she chose her words carefully. "You said you didn't like staying at the extended stay, but it's all you can afford, and I don't knock you for that. I swear I don't. Everyone has a story, and I don't know that man, and I'm not trying to judge, but . . ."

"But what?"

"But he's driving a Porsche truck staying there? Maybe it is just temporary, but that would be all the more reason for him to stay somewhere a little nicer. I'm not knocking where you have to stay for now, and I can admit your room is clean and better than many other places, but he can't have his shit all the way together staying there. You have enough on your plate. Any man you date needs to bring something to the table."

Lauren stared out of the window. Lakesha had invited her out for food and drinks, and she was treating. Lauren looked good and felt good with her new hairstyle and her press-on nails. She had been excited to tell Lakesha about Neville, but she had just ruined it that fast. Lakesha saw her friend's change in attitude, and she felt terrible.

"I'm sorry, Lauren. I'm not trying to rain on your parade, and you did say he's moving soon. Maybe he does have it together. I'm not shit for judging that man. Maybe he wanted to put all his money into the new place and didn't mind staying there. There could be a bunch of shit I don't know. I checked myself, and I'm going to do better." She smiled at her friend, but Lauren still looked defeated.

It never failed. Every time she got excited about something, it would always be short-lived. Lakesha had burst her bubble in only a matter of seconds.

"Has he asked you out?" Lakesha decided to keep probing.

"No," Lauren mumbled, and Lakesha sighed.

"Babe, I'm an ass, okay? You looking all cute with your hair and nails and were just blushing over there. Don't let me ruin that for you. I want more than anything to see you happy."

"It's no big deal. You're probably right. He just got Assad's ball for him one day, and he's taken a liking to him ever since. He saw me in the car crying because I was having a bad day. Assad needed new shoes, and I was just at my wit's end. He asked me what was wrong and gave me $500."

That comment got a rise out of Lakesha's eyebrows. "Okay, now, wait a minute. You should have led with that information. This stranger gave you $500 for Assad? You either better be really careful, or you better pop that pussy for a real nigga."

Lauren smiled at her friend's comment, but she also shook her head at the fact that the tune had changed so suddenly after the mention of money. She knew her friend only had her best interest at heart, however. Lakesha was right. Lauren was broke as hell and didn't need a man in her space who was doing as bad as she was. But she knew that Neville wasn't broke. He just didn't give her broke-nigga vibes.

"I doubt I'm his type. I saw him with a woman when we were doing laundry one day, and she was drop-dead gorgeous with an amazing body. Shit, her outfit and shoes combined probably cost more than I make in half a year."

Lakesha frowned. "Okay, and? Listen, you're having some financial problems, but what does that have to do with you as a person? I commend you for not being one of those women who will spend her last dime on material shit. You always put Assad and your responsibilities first, and you're drop-dead gorgeous yourself. Don't sleep on yourself. You're a natural beauty. You don't need weave, makeup, lashes, or any extras to be fine. If that nigga can't see that, then it's his loss. But I love you with your hair done. I think you should keep it up and give that ponytail a rest. Please."

Lauren giggled. "I'll see, but I won't make any promises."

When Lauren picked up Assad from school, she knew he was probably starving, so she had a snack for him in the car. She took him to the park and let him run and play for an hour, then headed back toward the hotel to cook them dinner. Once Assad ate, did his homework, and bathed, she knew he'd be out like a light. Since she still had some of the money that Neville had given her, she decided that Saturday morning, she would take Assad to breakfast for a mommy-and-son date. Being able to do little things like that for him made her smile.

Neville pulled up as they got out of the car at the extended stay, and Lauren's stomach began to feel funny. He really had an effect on her that she wasn't used to. It had been so long since she was attracted to or dealt with a man. She almost felt like she had forgotten how to deal with the opposite sex, but there really was no dealing with Neville. He showed more interest in Assad than he did her. She knew it would be rude not to speak after what he'd done for her, so she waited for him to get out of his vehicle.

"What's up?" he asked her before looking down at Assad. "Okay, Li'l Man, I like those kicks. Those are fly."

Assad beamed with pride. He was very young, but he could still recognize that Neville had nice things. He wore the kinds of clothes and shoes that Assad wanted to wear, so his compliment meant everything. He felt cool, and that was evident by the massive grin on his face.

"Thank you. My mommy bought them. She bought me two pairs of shoes."

"You're a lucky little man." Neville smiled at him before looking back up at Lauren.

He could see that she'd gotten her hair and nails done, but it was nothing major. It's not like she had gone out and dropped hundreds of dollars on wigs or bundles. He respected that she took the money and did what she was supposed to do for her son and did minimal for herself. That made Neville want to help her even more. For the life of him, he couldn't understand why he suddenly wanted to save this woman and her son. Maybe it was so that Lauren and Assad would have the chance he always wanted for his mother and himself.

His mother was a very smart woman who had gotten pregnant while off in college. Her parents wanted her to have an abortion to continue her education, but she refused. So they cut her off completely. She ended up dropping out of school and going to work cleaning houses. Neville had never known who his father was, and his mother never spoke about it. So all they had for the longest was each other . . . until she got hooked on drugs.

"You look nice," he complimented Lauren. She had on a black sundress and those same flip-flops. But her toenails were painted a soft pink, and he knew that if she could genuinely spoil and pamper herself, she'd be something serious. It didn't matter to him how plain she was. Neville went after the women he did because he wanted what they had. It had been awhile since he dealt with a woman for anything other than greed. He didn't date for love. He dated for a come-up. Women did that shit every day. So, if a woman was wealthy but didn't have the cutest face, Neville could get past that for the bigger picture. On the other hand, if he dated for looks and personality, Lauren would surely be on his radar.

"Thank you," she smiled. "Um, I'm about to go cook for me and Assad. Something quick like pasta. I don't know if you've eaten or if you cook or what, but if you'd like, I can bring you a plate." Lauren didn't want him to think she was pushing up on him. She just wanted to do something kind because he'd been nice to her.

"I haven't eaten since earlier, so that would be good. Thank you."

"Great! Give me about an hour and a half."

"My mommy can cook really, really, really, *really*, good," Assad bragged, making Neville and Lauren laugh.

"I can't wait to taste her food then because if you said it, I believe it." Neville smiled at Assad, winked at Lauren, and headed for the door.

Lauren tried to keep the smile off her face as she headed up to her room with Assad talking a mile a minute. She only offered to do something nice for him because that's how she could pay him back. It's not like he'd asked her out on a date or anything, so she couldn't understand why she was so happy.

In the room, Assad sat at the small table, and Lauren helped him with his homework while she cooked. Assad was right. She *could* cook. Lauren could cook her ass off, but she found herself trying to be extra careful and ensure everything was perfect with this meal. She wanted to impress Neville, and she knew it. There was no need to lie about it.

When she finished cooking, Lauren fixed their plates, and they sat down, talked, and ate. When they were done, she cleaned the small kitchen area and fixed a plate for Neville.

"Can I come with you to take Neville his food?" Assad asked.

"Yes, you can, and then it's shower time when we get back. You can watch thirty minutes of TV after that. Then it's story time and bedtime. Cool?"

"Cool."

Lauren smiled at her son, and they walked hand in hand to Neville's room. When he answered the door, Lauren saw that he had changed into some gray sweatpants and a white tank top, and her eyes darted over his muscles and slid down to that juicy dick print. Her knees almost buckled, and she snatched her gaze away and met his eyes.

"Um, here you go. I put garlic bread on the plate as well."

Neville had peeped her eyeing his package, and he wanted to laugh, but he kept it together. "Thank you. I really appreciate it. You saved me from having to eat yet another night of takeout."

"It's no problem. Anytime I cook, you can have a plate. I don't mind."

"I appreciate that." Neville looked down at Assad. "Was it good, Li'l Man?"

"It was delicious!"

Neville and Lauren laughed, and she said her goodbyes.

Two hours later, she was cuddled up in bed with her son. Her chin rested atop his head. As she talked to God with closed eyes, she felt tears forming. She knew her life could be much worse, but Lauren was ready for a break. The desire to get ahead and live the good life, even if only for a short time, burned inside her like a fire. *God, can I at least have a year before going back to scraping and scrambling?* She prayed harder than she had in a very long time because she just needed some relief.

At one time, Lauren always prayed for a husband. She just felt a good man would be the answer to her problems. He would come along and take a liking to Assad. He'd propose to her and let her have a much-needed break while he paid all the bills. Shit, at this point, she didn't even mind going half with a man if she had to, but she wanted a provider, someone financially stable that would allow her to get on her feet without the pressures of life. However, it seemed that wasn't in the cards for her, so she stopped praying for a husband. Now, she wanted doors to open for her. She needed a good job with benefits, weekends off, and some financial security.

If she could make two times more than what it cost her to live every month, she'd have plenty of cushion left over for savings and treating herself and Assad . . . just to experience shopping for new furniture and clothing, to pay her bills on time every month. Her mind went from being financially secure to Neville. He would have been the perfect fit for her fantasy. A provider that liked her son and took care of them. He was certainly someone that she wouldn't mind waking up beside every morning. She got so lost in her dreams about Neville that she drifted off.

Chapter 6

When Sherri handed Neville all the information he needed to access his new CPNs, he wanted to kiss her smack-dab on the lips. She had come through and saved his life—four new numbers, with two having credit scores over 800. Sherri was an older, Black woman who had spent years working in finance at three different banks, and she currently worked for an accounting firm. Neville didn't know exactly how she got the numbers with tradelines already listed, and he didn't care. He knew the information was probably stolen from deceased people, or maybe they were alive and just selling their info for a profit. Either way, it didn't make a bit of difference. He was about to come up.

The first thing he was going to do was look for an apartment. Then the credit card that he would have Simone add him to, he would use to start building one of the CPNs that was clear. He would use that number to max out on furnishing his new place and going on a much-needed vacation.

Now it was time to grab some IDs to match the fake names he would attach to the CPNs, so he hit his boy Black to make that happen ASAP. He hoped that the next three or four nights at the extended stay hotel would be a thing of the past.

Neville left Black's and went to view a townhome that was more his speed. He took in the manicured lawn and the garages attached to the townhome. It was in a newly developed upscale community. Neville fell in love with the modern, newly renovated townhome, the white granite marble countertops, and the shiny new chrome appliances. Neville liked that there were three floors, and the master bedroom was on the third floor, with a bathroom and a sitting room. The second floor had two bedrooms and a bathroom, and the living room, kitchen, laundry room, and a half bath were downstairs. He didn't blink when the leasing agent told him the rent was $4,400 a month. Neville completed the application with his new ID and CPN number, and the agent told him to give her a few minutes, and she should have a decision for him.

Neville wasn't worried about not being approved for the place. On the contrary, he was so confident that he would get the town house that he pulled out his phone while he sat on the plush couch in the nicely decorated clubhouse and started looking for furniture to purchase. He had just ordered an Italian leather living room set made when Chelsea walked over to him with a big smile. That told him she would be getting a nice commission from renting him the town house.

"I have great news, Mr. Barnes. You were approved for

the unit. You can sign the lease and get the keys as soon as you pay the deposit. Since the unit is brand-new, we don't have to wait for anyone to move out, and it's already clean. The lights and water are already on. We just ask that once you sign the lease, you get everything switched over to your name. If you have the deposit today, you can move in as early as tomorrow."

Neville rubbed his hands. "That's great news, and I definitely have the deposit and the first month's rent."

It would take some time for the living room set to be delivered, but that didn't matter. As long as he had a bed to sleep in, he would be fine, and as soon as he signed the lease, Neville was going to shop for a bedroom set that could be delivered the following day. It would be his last day at the extended stay, for sure. When all the paperwork was complete, he left the leasing office, whistling.

His phone rang, and he saw that Simone was calling. Neville had gotten enough out of her. She had business credit, and as soon as he got situated, he would set up a business account and have her exchange some tradelines for him. Personal credit was lucrative, but business credit was the next level. You could get four times the amount of credit lines for a business versus personal credit. He didn't want to be too greedy because the last time he had done that, shit really backfired on him. But he couldn't resist all the money he knew he could stack with a strong business credit line. Besides, if he started ignoring her now, she might get suspicious, so he answered.

"Hey, beautiful. What's good with you?"

"Hi, Neville," she sniffed. "I'm not feeling well. You know it's that time of the month, and my fibroids are really killing me. I've been hurting and crying for the past few hours. I've cried so much that I have a headache. I could really use some company right now."

There was no way he was about to let her mood bring him down. He had considered inviting her to help him shop for his new home accessories.

"Damn, babe, I would love nothing more than to hold you right now, but I'm actually in South Carolina on a business trip. I'll be here for another two days, but as soon as I touch back down in Charlotte, it's all about you. I want to take you out on a nice date, take you home, rub your feet, give you a massage, and kiss every inch of that gorgeous body," he stated in a sexy voice.

"I can't wait. I need that right now. I'd drive to South Carolina to see you if I didn't have work tomorrow. Hitting the highway would clear my mind."

"I'm in back-to-back meetings, and when I'm not in meetings, I'm visiting different sites and meeting with the foremen and the crew. So I wouldn't be able to give you the time you deserve if you came here, but please believe I got you when I get back."

"I'm going to hold you to that."

"Okay, babe. Later."

Neville ended the call and tossed the phone on the passenger seat of his vehicle. Simone and most women were under the impression that he was an architect. They always felt he was a good catch because he had a rewarding, successful career and lived a life that screamed he'd be a great provider. Even successful women wanted to be pampered. Neville did just enough to sell them a dream, and then he'd always come up with a sob story about how he ended up in a bad business deal and lost a large amount of money or how his drug-addicted sister wiped out his bank account. He had stories for days, and the women he wowed never minded holding him down and footing the bill while he got himself together. He'd get what he could and then ghost them.

It took Neville almost two hours to find a bedroom set that could be delivered the following day, and he also stopped by HomeGoods and TJ Maxx and got a few things for the new place. He'd hit Macy's, Belk's, and a few other stores that sold home décor and essentials the next day.

When he arrived at the extended stay, he sighed as he saw Lauren standing at her car with the hood up. That woman just couldn't catch a break. He got out of his truck and looked at her weary face.

"What's wrong with it?" he asked as he walked toward her.

"I think I need a new battery," her bottom lip quivered, and he knew she was on the verge of tears.

"Lauren," Neville couldn't believe what he was about to say or do. He had never in his life done anything like this.

She turned to face him, and he shook his head. Still in disbelief, he decided not to back out now. "I need to talk to you about something serious. I prefer to do it in the car rather than out in the open."

She looked at him curiously. What could he have to talk to her about? If he were about to proposition her for sex or something, he would get a piece of her mind. She was already frustrated and not in the mood. He had given her money, but he made it clear that she didn't owe him anything. He didn't need to change his tune now because, even though she needed a new battery for her car, she wouldn't have sex with him to get it.

Rather than voicing her concerns, she simply got into

her car and watched as he got in on the passenger side. Then Neville looked over at Lauren. "What I'm about to tell you, I've never shared with anyone. We don't know each other, and if you do not feel what I'm about to offer you, you can say that, and it won't be any sweat off my back. I just ask that you hear me out and look at the situation with an open mind."

Lauren stared at him blankly. Her mouth was dry, and her palms were sweaty. She was willing to bet money that she didn't have that he was about to ask her for a sexual favor. When she didn't reply, he continued.

"I know someone, and they give me CPN numbers. I use a number when applying for credit cards, apartments, buying homes, cars, applying for loans—the whole nine. It's pretty much just like getting a new Social Security number with no debt attached to it, and the credit score will always be good, even though the scores can vary. So I have a number I can give you, and you can use it to change your situation if that's something you want to do."

Lauren was interested but unsure. What if she went and applied for something, and they told her the number was no good or denied her anyway? "Is that illegal?" she asked, but she felt she already knew the answer.

"It's not exactly legal if you use a different name and technically assume a new identity. But if you use your real name and birthdate, you should be good. Just make sure you don't use any of your previous addresses. You don't want to connect it to your old credit accounts. And as long as you plan on paying off the bills you create, you won't have to worry about anything illegal.

"Trust me; this is something rich white folks do all the fucking time. I've lived in an expensive-ass high-rise, and they didn't blink twice when I used the number. I just got approved for a newly constructed townhome, and I was approved in minutes.

"There is always a risk with these types of things, but most times, you can get what you need to get with no issues. If you decide to use the number, my advice would be to apply for loans and credit cards and get as much cash as possible. Get you and Li'l Man a place to live and a decent car, and don't look back. Keep working your ass off and doing what you must do so that when the money runs out, you can maintain whatever you bought—no need to get used to living a certain way only to have it come back to this. When I've used a CPN number all that I can, I just get another one.

"If this isn't something that you want to keep doing, I suggest you have a plan. Normally, people can charge anywhere from $1,500 and up for one of these numbers, but I'm giving you this for you and Li'l Man."

Lauren nodded. He had given her a lot to process and think about. Normally, she would never do anything illegal and risk her freedom, but here this man was telling her this was how he had all his nice things. Lauren didn't need a flashy car or an expensive high-rise, but she did want to move her son to better conditions. She wanted to live her life without worrying about money every second of every day.

Lauren wanted to say no badly. She wanted to tell Neville that she couldn't risk doing anything to lose her son, but the word wouldn't leave her mouth. Her tongue felt heavy when she tried to speak, and all she could do was look at him for a moment. Finally, Lauren opened her mouth. "Thank you."

"It's no problem. I want to see you doing good things, and I know it makes you happy to make your son happy. Take this opportunity and turn your life around."

Neville gave Lauren the CPN number, and he also gave her his phone number. "Let me know if you have any issues. As I said, I got approved for my place, so this will be my last night here."

Neville exited her car, and Lauren stared after him for a few moments. She wasn't sure what had just happened, but she was scared *and* excited at the same time. She had never been a big risk taker. Lauren knew without a shadow of a doubt that if she went to prison, Lakesha would raise Assad, but just the thought of losing her son made tears spring to her eyes. That almost made Lauren get rid of the number and forget the silly notion of being a part of this scam, but then she looked up at her raised hood. A battery would run her almost $100. Lauren was so tired of her back being knocked against the wall that she wanted to scream at the top of her lungs. The longer she sat in the car and thought about the fact that she was broke as hell, and she had a meal ticket in her hands, the more she was with it. Fuck it, she was going to use the number, and whatever happened, happened.

Chapter 7

Lauren wanted to roll her eyes badly, but she didn't. One of the tables in her section had called her over four times in the past two minutes. She had been at work for four hours, and so far, she only had $60 in tips. It wasn't terrible, but she had spent all the money she had getting a battery for her car and paying someone to put it in. Then when she started the car, she realized that the tank was empty, and her last $10 went to her gas. The table of three obnoxious guys was getting on her last nerve, and she bet they wouldn't even tip. Regardless of her feelings, Lauren walked over to the table with a fake smile plastered on her face.

"How can I help you?"

"These fries are cold as hell." One of the guys pushed his plate toward her. "I want some fresh ones, and since I have to wait, I want a fresh burger too."

"Coming right up. Sorry about that," Lauren grabbed the plate and walked away. Once her back was turned, she rolled her eyes.

After taking the plate back into the kitchen, she eased out of the back door for some fresh air. She hated this place with a passion. Pulling her phone from her apron pocket, she checked her notifications and messages. With her back pressed against the building, she saw two new emails. That made Lauren curious because she had made fake email addresses when applying for anything using the CPN number.

She clamped her hand over her mouth when she saw the first message. She stared at the message for the longest time, reading the words repeatedly, and no matter how many times she read them, she still couldn't believe that it was real. She'd been approved for a credit card with a limit of $25,000. That was more money than she'd ever had access to in her life, and what was even better, they'd already given her a number in case she wanted to purchase things online before the physical card came in the mail. Lauren couldn't believe it. It worked! Her hands were trembling with excitement as she closed out of that message and went to the next one. Lauren squealed when she saw that she'd been approved for another credit card with a limit of $18,000. Just like that, she now had access to $43,000.

Lauren wanted to take off her apron, toss it onto the ground, get in her car, and never look back, but that wouldn't be smart. She couldn't quit her job just yet. Lauren had no intention of asking Neville for another CPN number, so she had to make this one count. Quitting her job just yet wasn't an option. As soon as she got off work, she would apply for an apartment. Lauren wanted a decent place to live for Assad and her. That was her main priority. Maybe she'd even get another car. She reminded herself that she had to slow down. She couldn't do too much too soon. With a big smile, she slid her cell phone back into her apron and returned to wait on her obnoxious-ass customers. She was in such a good mood that not even they could ruin it for her. Lauren's brain was working overtime to figure out how to make this CPN move her best move. She didn't just want to go shopping and buy some new things here and there. She wanted Assad's and her lives to change for the better. There was no way she would blow this amazing opportunity that had been presented to her by a man she barely even knew.

IT WAS HARD FOR LAUREN TO KEEP HER COMPOSURE AS she walked through the apartment where the leasing agent was taking her on a tour. The spacious two-bedroom unit had two bathrooms, and what she really loved about the place was the park within walking distance from the very unit she was looking at. The stark white walls, the smell of fresh paint, and the stainless steel appliances made Lauren want this to be her new home so badly. She wanted to squeal and jump for joy, but she acted as if she weren't impressed as the leasing agent tried to sell her on the place. The thought of decorating the apartment and surprising her son made her say a silent prayer. She knew that maybe God wasn't pleased with her because, technically, she was stealing, but she was trying to provide a better life for Assad, and she refused to be sorry for that.

"What do you think?" Kaylha finally turned to ask her when they finished the tour.

"I love it. The apartment is nice, and I love the park. What do I need to apply?"

"Just your driver's license, Social Security number, and proof of income. We use a third-party company to do the credit and background check so that you can hear back today, no later than tomorrow. It just depends on how busy they are. Also, there is a $75 application fee and a $125 administrative fee."

"That's no problem. I can handle that. I want to apply."

Lauren walked with Kaylha back to the leasing office with a racing heart. It would be cruel for her to have gotten her hopes all up just for something to happen where she was denied the apartment. But if she were, she'd just try again. After all, she'd gotten the credit cards with ease. She had planned to apply for a few more before all the inquiries and cards affected the credit score attached to the CPN. If the score was indeed over 800, she should certainly be able to get a few more things. The next account she applied for would be for a furniture store so that she could decorate her new place. Lauren was so excited that the guilt she felt from doing anything wrong quickly faded away.

When she finished the application, she passed it to Kaylha along with the cash to pay for the fees. She had made $300 at work, and though applying for the apartment would take most of that, she didn't care. If she got the apartment and no longer had to pay for the extended stay, she could use everything she had made from the restaurant to pay her bills. In the meantime, she would devise another way to make money. The restaurant wouldn't cut it anymore if she got approved for the apartment that was $1,800 a month. She knew she could have tried to find a cheaper place, but Lauren convinced herself that she and her son deserved to live in that neighborhood in that apartment.

She hadn't been as happy as she now felt in such a long time. Even if she didn't get approved for the apartment, she was glad to have the two credit cards coming.

On her way to pick up Assad from school, Lauren passed a vacant space for lease, and she got an idea. It came to her out of nowhere, and she wondered if she could pull it off. She knew she needed to focus on one thing at a time, but this was her and Assad's future. She knew she couldn't blow this.

LAKESHA LOOKED AROUND LAUREN'S NEW APARTMENT IN awe. She had been watching Assad a lot for Lauren over the past five days while she did a lot of extra hours. Lauren had worked six days in a row and hadn't worked anything less than ten hours each day. Lakesha knew her friend was trying to move, but how in the heck did five days of working long hours turn into *this*? Lauren's new apartment was super nice and in a great area. The living room was decked out with a lovely gray sectional, a glass coffee table, two end tables, and a large rug, and she had paid the Geek Squad to come hang her sixty-inch television on the wall. Just the living room alone impressed Lakesha, but when she saw Assad's bedroom, her eyebrows lifted.

The child had a full-sized bed with two dressers and two nightstands. He had a huge toybox in the corner filled with toys, and his closet was filled with clothes and shoes that Lakesha had never seen before. Even the bathrooms were decorated nicely, and Lauren's bedroom was nice as hell. Lakesha wanted all the tea. She leaned up against the wall as Lauren poured them glasses of wine.

"This place is really nice, Lauren. I'm so happy for you and Assad, and I'm super proud of you, but how did you get the money for all this?" She was under the impression that Lauren was waiting to hear back from low-income housing. She didn't want her friend to bite off more than she could chew and find herself once again getting evicted. She didn't even know how her friend got this nice-ass place when she already had one eviction on her credit. Lakesha's credit was good, and she didn't want for anything thanks to her man, but she still wanted Lauren to put her up on game.

Lauren loved Lakesha like a sister, but she just wasn't willing to tell anyone that she had gained all these things illegally. It didn't seem like a smart move to her. The six days in a row that she worked, Lauren had managed to make a little over $2,000 in tips, and just like that, before she even moved in, she had the rent money secured for the next month. She had paid the first month's rent and the security deposit with money from the credit cards, but she knew that wouldn't last. Lauren was waiting to hear back from the bank about a loan of $15,000 that she had applied for. She was going to milk that CPN number.

"I have to be honest; Neville helped me." Lakesha's eyes widened because that was the last thing she had expected to hear. "Let me clarify that I busted my ass this past six days at work to get next month's rent money. I plan to stay ahead. I don't want to always depend on someone to help me. I'm taking three days off to get settled and spend some time with my son, and then it's right back to the grind. All I needed was a head start, and I promise I won't let my son down again."

Lakesha didn't know what to say. "You just met this guy, Lauren. Does he need a place to live? I mean, this apartment isn't cheap, and this is some nice-ass furniture. He helped you to get all of this? Is there something you *aren't* telling me? Have you slept with this man?"

"You know I've never been the type to sleep with men for money, but I'll be honest with you, Lakesha. Neville is fine as hell, and if he had offered me all of this for a little romp around the bedroom, I might have taken it. But no, I haven't slept with him. I told you he's a nice guy, and he likes Assad. He just wanted to help me."

Surely Lauren wasn't this naive. "Lauren, I don't know what this Neville character does for a living, but I'm no stranger to dating drug dealers. And I know plenty of men that will give women money for apartments, cars, and the whole nine, but that's because there is something in it for them too. Drug dealers don't get houses and cars in their own name. They find some woman to do it for them, and it's all fine and well . . . until they break up, or he gets locked up, or killed, and she can't pay for things anymore. So, men spending money fast on a woman, no, that's not unheard of. But it's unheard of for him to do it just because he's a nice guy and likes your son. So what's in it for him?"

Lauren sipped her wine. She knew Lakesha wasn't going to drop the issue. "Can we please not dwell on this? I will tell you that I don't think Neville sells drugs, but he makes his money fast. And I'm smart enough to know that most people who make their money fast don't value it or respect it like a hardworking person. They live by the motto that whatever they spend, they can make it right back, and I think Neville has that kind of mind-set. But I can assure you that my name is on the lease, and my son and I are the only ones who will be living here. I haven't even seen Neville since he gave me what I needed to get this place."

Lakesha stared at her friend as she sipped her wine. There was something really strange about this Neville character. Lakesha wasn't against her friend getting her bones jumped. She desperately needed a good man, and Lakesha wanted that for her, but Assad was her heart. She couldn't bear to see him suffer in any way because Lauren got desperate and let the wrong man into their lives. She didn't know a thing about this Neville except he was fine, and fine men did fuck boy shit all the time. Before meeting her current boyfriend, Lakesha was with a man who relentlessly spoiled her and beat her mercilessly. She couldn't stand by and let that kind of man get a hold of Lauren, especially since she would look at him like a savior for taking her out of the situation that she was in. She would feel like she owed him something and stick around way longer than she needed to. Lakesha knew very well how the cycle went.

"Okay, there is nothing I can say because you're grown. I'm super excited for you, and I hope this Neville person is a stand-up guy. You and Assad deserve the best. Neither one of you should be subjected to bullshit from a liar or a manipulator . . . or a man trying to control you with money."

Lauren smiled at her overly protective friend and was glad she had someone in her corner to look out for her.

Lakesha made her feel loved. Lauren placed her wineglass down and hugged her friend tight. "Thank you so much for everything you've ever done for Assad and me. We love you and appreciate you. And thank you for having my best interest at heart. You know I love my son more than anything, and I only accepted Neville's help because Assad deserves this. The smile on his face when he saw his room had me bawling my eyes out. I finally did it. I finally gave my son what he deserved, and it will only get better from here."

Lakesha still had her reservations but decided not to voice any more of them. Lauren looked so happy, and Assad was having a ball in his new room, playing on his new iPad. Lakesha still wanted to know what was up but decided to drop it for now and celebrate with her friend. The interrogation could resume later.

Chapter 8

With all his new accounts, Neville was all the way back on his shit. After meeting Amoye at a bar near his new home and getting her full rundown, he knew she would be a sweet lick. She was really an overshare bear and told him everything about her marriage in the first few hours. Now, here she was back at his place, proving just how much she needed a side nigga in her life.

"Ummmm," he moaned as she deeply throated his member. Finally, Neville lifted his hips and began to fuck her mouth, almost choking her.

She placed her hands flat on his thighs and took the thrusts like a big girl, even when the head of his dick tapped the back of her throat. Amoye gagged a few times but relaxed her throat muscles and showed out for Neville. Spit dripped off her chin as he grabbed a handful of her hair and grunted as his seeds shot down her throat.

"Fuck," he roared as she hummed on his dick and sucked up every drop like a starved freak. Neville was breathing hard and trying to compose himself, and she was still sucking and licking like she didn't want to part ways with his dick.

She finally removed her mouth from his tool and smiled at Neville. They had already had one round of sex, and when Neville was still hard after he came, she took him into her mouth and sucked him into orgasm number two. She wanted to make sure to leave him with his balls drained, and she could go home and not care about the fact that her husband was more than likely going to come up with another excuse not to have sex with her.

Amoye's husband was seven years her senior, and it seemed like each year, their sex life had gotten worse and worse. Finally, about seven months ago, it turned nonexistent. They hadn't had sex one time in seven months, and no one could make Amoye believe that he wasn't having an affair. She cared but not as much as she would have if she hadn't just met Neville.

Neville stood up and picked up his jeans off the floor. His time in the hotel room with Amoye had been fun, but he had things to do. He was planning to give this new sexual relationship a little time before he hit her up for a few AUs and possibly a cosign on his new business account he had Sherri help set up for him. The good thing with Amoye was, since she was married, he wouldn't have to worry too much about blowback after he quit fucking with her. In his experience, most married women kept their shit quiet because of the embarrassment and not wanting to be exposed. The other big bonus was she couldn't request to be taken on dates or for him to spend much time with her. Right now, all she wanted was dick, and he would give her plenty of that as long as the money to come matched.

"When am I going to see you again?" Amoye asked while lying on the bed on her knees, looking up at Neville with a hopeful expression on her face.

He walked over, leaned down, and tongued her down so passionately that she moaned into his mouth. That was Neville's good-money kiss, but Amoye didn't know any better.

"Soon," Neville promised her and tapped the tip of her nose.

"All you have to do is hit my line, and I'll be there. The way you put it down in the bedroom, I can't see any man in his right mind not wanting to slide up in that every night," he stroked her ego.

She grinned.

"You won't ever have to beg me to get that pussy." Neville was laying it on thick, and it was working. Amoye was smiling so hard he was surprised her cheeks weren't hurting. Neville smiled back, but this was due to him thinking about the cash he would have after he had her take out a huge home equity loan on that big-ass house she shared with her husband.

"You certainly know how to flatter a woman." Amoye hadn't stopped smiling and blushing yet.

"It's easy when she deserves it." Neville placed a soft peck on her lips before putting on his shoes and leaving the hotel room. He had work to do when he got home.

LAUREN KNEW SHE WAS ABOUT TO GET HIT WITH SOME bullshit when she saw her manager walking over to her with a red face. Marty was an overweight white man that constantly gave her grief. The only thing that kept her going these days was that she knew if she hung in there just a tad bit longer and worked really hard, she'd be able to kiss the restaurant goodbye, and her pockets wouldn't suffer because of it.

She had been in her apartment for two weeks and had been approved for three more credit cards, a business loan, and a personal loan. She did not doubt that she could make things happen for her and Assad with those things. However, she was still working five days a week. Lauren refused to allow herself to relax. She wasn't out of the woods just yet. Her new apartment was expensive, and she needed to be good for the year. She never wanted to go through the trauma of being evicted again, and as much as Neville had changed her life, she didn't want to become addicted to using CPN numbers. Being greedy would be a sure way for her to get caught.

"Lauren, do you mind staying an extra two hours? Unfortunately, Haley can't come in. Her kid is sick."

"No can do. I have an appointment that I can't miss. And I have a kid too. No one is ever willing to stay longer or come in earlier when I'm in a bind." Lauren wasn't ready to quit her job just yet, but she now had the confidence to be more open with sharing her grievances. She hated this job and was tired of pretending it wasn't a toxic work environment full of lazy manipulators. She was supposed to get off in an hour and wasn't staying a minute over that time.

Marty sighed in frustration. "Maybe I should just clean house and bring in a new staff that wants to work and doesn't have kids."

Lauren shrugged her shoulders as if it didn't matter to

her one way or another. "Then that would be discrimination, and I'm pretty sure it's illegal."

Marty stared at her momentarily, trying to figure out when and how she got so bold. Finally, rather than spewing any more threats, he decided to walk away. If she didn't want to stay, he couldn't make her. But the next time she begged for a longer shift, he'd be sure to deny her since she wanted to be selective about when she needed money. Deep down, it wasn't right, and Marty knew he was an asshole, but he didn't care.

The restaurant was packed, and that last hour flew by. Soon, Lauren was leaving with a pocket full of tips. She deposited the money in the bank and headed to her destination. She was so excited that she smiled the entire way to the space she was about to lease. Lauren had used some of the money from the business loan to pay the rent on the space for three months. She had the bright idea to open a content studio and knew she'd do pretty well with all the photographers without studios and social media influencers around. So she would start off charging people $150 an hour to come in and use her studio for photoshoots, social media reels, to create YouTube content, etc. The space was pretty big, and she planned to stage five different areas inside.

One area would be set up with couches across from each other, and it would be a great setup for people who wanted to film content for podcasts. Another area would be arranged like a living room with couches, a recliner, an area rug, a coffee table, décor, etc. The third area would have a bar, barstools, and liquor bottles in the background, like a real bar. The fourth area would be set up with a bed, two nightstands, and a floor-length mirror, and lastly, the fifth area would be like an office with a desk, chair, book-shelf, computer, etc.

After she paid the rent for three months and priced everything she'd need for the staging, factored in the cost of the website, and got the utilities turned on, Lauren would only have $1,500 left over from the business loan, but that was fine. She'd use that for the rent and utilities until it ran out.

When Lauren arrived at the location and got the keys from the realtor, her eyes filled with tears. Her life had changed in a matter of weeks. Things that she used to dream about had come to fruition, and she was elated. However, there were many times that she had to pinch herself to see if she was dreaming. Lauren had felt an influx of emotions over the past few weeks. She'd be insanely happy for hours, and then out of nowhere, fear would grip her like a vice. All of the positive changes in her life felt too good to be true, and she was waiting for the day it would all be snatched away from her.

She tried to tell herself that she was being dramatic and that Neville had assured her that it would be okay. From what she could tell, he had fallen on his luck once, and that didn't last long at all. And the fact that he shared his secret with her and gave her a chance where there was no other way, Lauren would never forget that. She would never forget him.

edric turned his chair around and round as he spoke on the phone to one of his colleagues in another location. He was working on quite a few cases, and while all of them were important, there was one that he wanted to solve ASAP. Cedric's ears perked up at the sound of the notification alerting him that he had an email. His eyes scanned the words on the screen while his coworker talked a mile a minute.

"Got him!" Cedric glared at the email he'd just gotten. One of the CPN numbers he'd flagged came back with several hits, and something told him it was Neville. "Jake, let me call you back. I finally got a hit on this case I've been working on."

Cedric didn't even wait for the man to reply as he ended the call and entered information into the correct database.

"Son of a bitch." Cedric clapped his hands happily. He had never been more excited to bring someone down.

Of course, there were extremely violent criminals out there who had done way worse things than Neville, but Cedric didn't appreciate how the man had stolen from his sister. That was some low-life, cowardly shit to do, and he didn't respect it. He could only imagine how many other poor, unsuspecting women Neville had stolen from, and Cedric wanted to be the one to see him get what he deserved. So he sat at the computer and did his research. He wanted all addresses, purchases, etc., associated with the list of CPN numbers.

Cedric glanced at his watch. It was ten after five, but he knew he wouldn't be leaving anytime soon. Not until he put a dent in this case. Neville had been roaming the streets doing dirt for too long. Cedric would be elated to watch him get handcuffed. He wanted his sister to testify and help put that bastard away. Cedric was going to try to find more of Neville's victims. The more people he had speaking out against the man, the better.

He sat at his desk and worked for hours to bring this whole ordeal to an end. All he had to do next was figure out when and where he would get his ass.

NEVILLE WALKED INTO THE RESTAURANT, UNSURE OF what he would find. However, he was pleasantly surprised when he saw Lauren standing before him, looking completely different. She had texted him earlier and asked him to meet her at a five-star restaurant, and he knew right then and there that she had indeed used the CPN number. He wasn't sure if she would, but Lauren would never be able to afford this kind of restaurant with her financial troubles.

Lauren stood in a beautiful red, sequined dress that stopped midthigh. She wore black heels, and her hair was full of body and bounce. Her short red nails matched the dress. He wondered if her toes were red too. She had undoubtedly indulged in self-care, and she was glowing. Lauren looked good, but more importantly, she looked happy. He guessed happiness was something that money *could* buy.

Neville went in for a hug. "You look really good." Lauren did clean up nice, and he was impressed that she hadn't gone out and blown her newfound riches on Gucci, Chanel, Prada, or any other high-end label, but she still looked damn good.

"Thank you. I invited you out just to say thank you. I can't begin to tell you how my life has changed since you gave me that number."

The hostess escorted the two to their seat before Neville could respond to Lauren's comment. Once he was sitting across from her, he gave her a head nod. "I'm glad you could use the number to your advantage. That's all I wanted for you to get on your feet. How is Li'l Man doing?"

A big smile crossed Lauren's face. "He is doing great. He has a new room full of nice new things. I'm hurt that he doesn't want to sleep with me anymore, but the smile that lit up his face when he saw his room was the greatest joy I have ever felt. I know it's not all about material things, but it feels damn good to spoil my child after he stayed down in the trenches for so long with me. Sometimes I could only afford to get him two or three gifts for Christmas, and it broke my heart."

"You're a great mother, Lauren. There is no shame in struggling. It happens to the best of us. The point is you never got comfortable with it, and you were always trying to climb out of it. On the real, I admire you and how you handle things so much."

"Wow, thank you so much for saying that. I've never felt like I've accomplished anything for anyone to admire."

"Are you kidding? You have held shit down for you and Assad when most women would have just given up. And they damn sure aren't good parents. That's why I don't have any kids. I've never met anyone I would trust or want to parent a child with." His compliments made Lauren feel even happier than she already felt, and she didn't think that was possible.

"Can I ask you something? And if it's none of my business, you can just tell me that."

"Sure, ask away, luv."

"How long have you been doing this? Again, if you don't mind me asking."

Neville was never going to let anyone in on all his business. Especially not the intricate details. But he would entertain her curiosity for a few.

"For a while. I won't lie. It's kind of addicting."

"It definitely is." Lauren giggled. "I have to tell myself all the time that this is it and not to go out and get more accounts."

"You still working at the restaurant?"

"I am for now. Tips have been excellent lately, and I'm not ready to walk away just yet. Thanks to the loans I've gotten and the credit cards, everything I make at work goes into my savings. I've never in my adult life had more than $500 in my savings account, and I would always run into some kind of a bind and have to withdraw the money after a month or two. It barely stayed in the account long enough to draw interest."

"That's the past. As I said, we all have a story to tell, so there's no shame in it. Just know that moving forward, you're going to have a new life, and you and Li'l Man will be straight." Lauren just smiled, and Neville wondered why she looked like she knew something he didn't. "What?"

"Nothing. I hope I don't sound desperate when I say this, but when I was back at the extended stay and a little on the plain side, I was far from your type, huh? I mean, I've seen the kind of women you date, and I don't fit the criteria at all."

Neville smiled and shook his head. "I'm a man that operates off hustle. Most things that I do are calculated. I rarely do anything just because, so dating isn't really something I do unless there is a purpose involved."

"Wait, so you're something like a gigolo?" He was fine and all, but Lauren would never take care of a man. Not even one that put her in the position to get money. It sounded like he was saying that he only dated women that he could get something out of, and if that were the case, it made sense that he never looked her way because she didn't have shit to offer him.

Neville laughed. "A gigolo? I don't charge women for sex. I'm not a male prostitute, but as I said, most of my moves are calculated."

"Why did you help me then? If your moves are calculated, what did you get from helping me?"

"I said most. I already told you why I helped you, and

from the way you said Li'l Man smiled when he saw his room and the way you were smiling when I walked in, then I did what I set out to do. Besides, you wouldn't want to date a man like me anyway."

"Why not?" she asked curiously. The waiter came over to take their drink orders, and she ordered a glass of wine.

"Because I'm not the settling down type, and you have Li'l Man. You need men in your life who will be a good example for him."

"That is true, but who said every man that entered my life would be someone that Assad had to meet? Mama gotta have a life too. I could just date. Without it being serious."

Neville smiled. She was too good for a nigga like him. She didn't need to get caught up in any of his bullshit, but if she wanted to have a little fun, that might be something that he was willing to do. "I hear you talking. A little fun, you said? When was the last time you dealt with anyone?" he asked curiously.

"It's been years. Honestly, when you're a single mother trying to work as much as you can, you don't want to spend too much time away from your kids, so you don't date much. Since Assad is in school now, that gives me a little more flexibility. I've tried to do breakfast dates and brunch dates, but many of these men don't have anything to offer but bullshit lies, games, and broken promises. So I gave up trying to have a friend and just embraced celibacy."

"Nothing wrong with that."

Neville and Lauren got to know each other a little better over dinner, and he asked her who Assad was with, and she said her friend Lakesha. "What time do you have to pick him up?"

Lauren was buzzed off three glasses of wine and inwardly prayed that he would ask to come home with her. And he did. Lauren was nervous when she drove back to her apartment with Neville behind her in his Porsche truck. She hadn't had sex in so long that despite the buzz from the alcohol she consumed at dinner, she was still slightly nervous. What if the sex was terrible, and he left and never called her again? That would be super embarrassing. Lauren pushed her reservations to the back of her mind and decided that sex was like riding a bike, and she would never forget how to do it. As long as he did what he was supposed to and turned her on, her body would react naturally, and the rest would come flooding back to her.

Inside the apartment, Lauren beamed with pride as Neville looked around in admiration. Every time she walked through the door, she almost cried. It was the nicest place she had ever lived in, and she hoped to be there for a while. The only way that she wanted to move was if she was moving into something bigger and better. She also felt extra good because she'd gotten her first booking for the content studio. A local photographer had booked the space for six hours, making her a grand total of $900 for one day. Not bad at all. Someone had also paid the deposit to spend two hours for a sweet sixteen photoshoot.

Neville wasn't a man that liked to waste time, so he walked over to Lauren and let his eyes trail over her body. "Take this off," he said with his eyes on her dress.

Lauren cleared her throat and did as he asked. She

didn't want to come across as nervous, but she was, and she wasn't the most confident regarding her body. However, she had fantasized about Neville many times, and now that she had the chance, she wasn't going to blow it. Lauren stood before him, clad only in her bra and panties, and Neville began placing a trail of kisses from her neck to her breasts. As his lips explored her body, he massaged one of her breasts, causing her to bite her bottom lip as electricity shot through her. It had been too long since she'd been touched by anyone other than herself. Lauren had a rose toy that she'd had to replace the batteries in five or six times. It had become her best friend.

Neville stared into her eyes before kissing her. He wanted to give her a warning. A warning not to get caught up and not to expect too much from him, but he didn't. Instead of saying what he was thinking, Neville placed his lips on hers and kissed her. Lauren's pussy grew moist from Neville's touch, and her body trembled anxiously. She had never wanted anyone as badly as she wanted him. The things he told her at dinner had changed her mind about him. He broke the kiss and grabbed her hand.

"Show me to the bedroom."

Lauren pulled him in the right direction, and when they were inside the bedroom, he pulled down her panties, and she stepped out of them. Usually, Neville worked overtime to please the women he sexed in bed because he knew that was the fastest way for them to let their guard down. It was Neville's job to make women fall in love with him, but he wanted to fuck Lauren crazy for different reasons. He didn't want to be too cocky with his thinking, but she deserved it. She was a good mother who was single and spent most of her time catering to her son. So Neville felt that it was only fitting he break her off with some dick so good, she'd be thinking about it for months to come. He guided her over to the bed and began to place wet kisses inside her thighs.

Neville watched her face contort as he rubbed her clitoris with his thumb. When she began to squirm and bite on her bottom lip, Neville knew that she was turned on and ready for him, but just to be sure, he inserted a finger into her opening and found her wet and sticky for him. Neville removed his finger and placed it in her mouth. Lauren maintained eye contact with him as she sucked her own juices off his finger. Neville's dick was harder than steel. He was ready to slide up in her. He undressed and handed her the condom. He loved the feel of a woman's soft hands rolling a rubber onto his shaft.

Lauren sat up and kissed the head of his dick before she opened the condom wrapper and removed the protection. When his dick was covered, he wasted no time pushing her back and entering her. Lauren was tight and wet, and he had to stifle a moan. He moved in and out of her slowly. He could fuck her hard and fast, or he could go slow and let her savor the moment. He had no clue how many times he'd actually have sex with Lauren, so he needed to make this time count.

Lauren lightly scratched his back as he slow-stroked her. The dick felt so good, and the way he hit her with slow strokes that went super deep had her toes curling and loud moans filling the room. Neville stroked her a little faster as he sucked on her earlobe.

"Neville," she moaned as she wrapped her arms around him and held his body tight. She never wanted this to be over. In her mind, Neville's dick was made for her. As he stroked her, she enjoyed the feel of him, his scent, and his touch.

"I'm about to come," she whispered, and he maintained his steady rhythm. Neville kissed Lauren, and she clenched her pussy muscles on his dick as she came.

He came shortly after her, and though she was completely satisfied, she hated when the moment ended. It had been the first time she had sex in a while, but he surely didn't disappoint. Neville smiled down at Lauren as he pulled out of her. Before he got up, he placed a kiss on her forehead. He was not even sure what the act of endearment was for. For Lauren, it was a beautiful sentimental act. It was late, so she wasn't going to get Assad. He would stay with Lakesha until morning, and for that reason, she wanted Neville to stay, but she refused to ask. Lauren just knew he was about to get dressed and leave, but to her surprise, he used the bathroom, discarded the condom, and slid right back into her bed.

The following day as she made her way out of the apartment to get Assad, Lauren's thighs were sorer than ever, but it was a pain that she enjoyed. She went three rounds with Neville, and her body felt it for sure. She was glad she had the day off, and after checking her website and seeing that she had four bookings for her content studio, Lauren was counting down the days until she could quit the restaurant.

Neville left an hour or so before she would, and when Lauren opened her front door, she was startled to see two men standing there. They weren't regular police officers. They looked like detectives.

"May I help you?" she asked as her heart palpated.

"Are you Lauren Woodruff?"

"Yes, I am."

"You're under arrest for identity theft and fraud. I won't put you in handcuffs, but I need you to lock your apartment and come with me, ma'am."

Chapter 10

L auren had never been more frightened in her life. As she sat in the interrogation room with the two detectives eyeing her like she'd fucked up, Lauren was shitting bricks. She knew this shit was too damn good to be true, and so it had been. She hadn't even been able to enjoy being financially stable for three full months before the rug had been snatched from underneath her. Would she end up being homeless again? Would they kick her out of her apartment? Freeze all the cards? Lauren was glad she had cash tucked away, but would it even be enough to post bond? Would she be broke after she posted the bond? All these thoughts ran through her mind, leaving her on the verge of tears. She knew Assad was good with Lakesha, but her son would surely miss her and want to know where she was if she remained away from him for too long. Just the thought of having to go to jail and leaving Assad made the tears that had formed in her eyes fall.

The detectives stared at her, taking in how afraid she

was. They could smell the fear oozing off her, and that's what they wanted. Lauren had broken the law, but Cedric didn't want her. Maybe she too was a victim caught up in Neville's spell as his sister had been. If she cooperated and gave him Neville, he'd see that she got to remain a free woman to raise her son and put her life back together. Cedric was disappointed when his digging led him to her and not to Neville. That's who he really wanted, and no one else would do.

"Where did you get the CPN number that you're using?" Cedric asked as he glared at a crying Lauren.

She wiped the tears from her face. Lauren wasn't necessarily from the streets and was green to many things, but she knew that snitching was frowned upon. Neville offered the number but didn't force her to take it. She had done that all on her own, so why bring him down?

"A f-friend gave it to me," she stammered. "I needed somewhere to live, and it was just explained to me that the number was like a Social Security number with a clean credit history attached. So I didn't think that it was anything I could go to jail for." She could only hope they bought her excuse.

"A friend, huh? You may not have known exactly what you were in possession of, but the person who gave you that number is far from a friend. They knew it was illegal when they gave it to you. If it were that simple and easy to use Social Security numbers that didn't belong to us, everyone would be doing it. It is very much illegal to obtain things under false pretenses. What's the name of the friend that gave you this number?"

"I-I just know her by Sarah. She was staying at the

extended stay hotel that me and my son were staying at. I don't know her last name."

Cedric frowned. "Sarah? Who in the hell is Sarah? Are you saying that you didn't get that number from a man named Neville?"

Lauren's heart raced, hearing that. They already knew about Neville. Fuck! She was technically lying to the police, and she knew that she was digging a hole for herself.

"No, I didn't. But look, using the number was on me. I did it. Is, um . . . Can I go to jail for that?"

The fear that her eyes held made Cedric aware that he could crack her if he remained persistent. "You have a son, right? Is his father around?"

Lauren felt light-headed. He knew way too much about her, and she was uncomfortable as fuck. How long had this man been investigating her? He knew about Assad? "Y-yes, I do have a son, and his father's dead."

"You have another family member that will take him in? Because the charges you're facing certainly carry a minimum of three years in prison."

If Lauren weren't sitting down, she would have fainted. She couldn't do three years in prison. Lauren couldn't even do three days away from Assad. No matter how scared she was, she still couldn't find it to give up Neville, and she didn't even know why. No one was more important than Assad. He was the only person she owed loyalty to, but Neville had helped her put more smiles on Assad's face in the past few weeks than she had in months. Neville had helped her. What they did may have been wrong, but it was the only way.

"Neville uses women. He's a con artist and a scammer. He gets them to let their guard down, then robs them blind. *Everything* that man has, has come off the backs of innocent women he took advantage of. That's the kind of sick fuck you're protecting?" Cedric spoke in a disgusted tone.

Lauren stammered over her words. She didn't know what to say. That didn't sound like the Neville who had helped her without barely even knowing her. But he had, in so many words, admitted to her that he wasn't a good guy, and he hadn't pursued her because she didn't have anything to offer him. Lauren was thrown for a loop. There was no way she wanted to leave her son and go to prison, but there was something in her that wouldn't allow her to give up Neville.

"L-like I said, I got the number from a woman named Sarah. I don't know anyone by the name of Neville." She could barely look Cedric in the eyes, and he knew she was lying.

"Give me a last name for this Sarah. A last name, a phone number, an address or something, or we're booking you," he stated angrily.

"I don't know." Tears ran down her cheeks, and had she been able to look at Cedric, she would know just how hard he was glaring at her. Mad was an understatement. He was livid.

Cedric looked over at his partner. "Take her to booking."

Lauren's world went dark. She would have to spend the night in jail. She may have to spend more nights in jail. She hadn't been allowed to use the phone, so she knew

Lakesha had no idea where she was, and she and Assad were probably worried sick.

"Can I use the phone?" she asked in a shaky voice.

"No," Cedric snapped. He wasn't playing by the rules. He didn't have to. Fuck her phone call. Since she wanted to play tough and not give up Neville, she would suffer. He'd let her use the phone eventually, but for now, she couldn't use shit. Lauren would sit in her cell and think about who she was protecting.

NEVILLE WAS IN LOS ANGELES, SITTING COURTSIDE AT A Lakers game, having the time of his life. He left Charlotte for a few days so he could have fun and relax for a while. Life was really good right now, and he was about to enjoy it to the fullest. However, the interaction between Lauren and him had him a bit confused. When he awoke the following day with her lying beside him, it just felt so natural. And now, here he was, 2,000 miles away, and she was still on his mind, blocking thoughts of guessing what she and Assad were probably doing today.

He glanced at the large crowd and caught the eye of a young woman sitting a few rows over. She had been eyeing him flirtatiously all night. It wasn't hard for Neville to detect that the groupie was trying to figure out who he was and how long his money was. So Neville decided the second time he caught her ogling him that she would be his entertainment for the night. During halftime, she got up out of her seat and boldly made her way over to him. The exotic beauty was Korean and Black; she was just the kind of arm candy Neville liked.

The Cartier watch on her wrist made him aware that she either had her own money or she had one hell of a sponsor. The diamonds in her ears and in her tennis bracelet were real, and she was dripping in Versace.

"These are quite some seats you have here," she stated coyly.

"Yeah, they are. The ones you have aren't too shabby, either."

"I come to all of the home games."

"Really? You know any of the players, or are you a lover of the sport?"

"Both. My cousin plays for the Lakers, but I've loved basketball since elementary school. My father is a retired coach."

So, she came from money. Neville nodded and looked her over as she stood before him in jeans that looked like a second layer of skin. "What's your name?" he inquired.

"Lexy. What's yours?"

"Neville, and I'm from North Carolina. I only flew in for a few days. I got here the day before yesterday, and my flight leaves tomorrow at 2:00 p.m." He subtly let her know he didn't have much time.

"Where are you staying?"

The look in her eyes made Neville aware that if she liked his answer, she'd accompany him for the night. He had just parted his lips to speak when his phone buzzed in his pocket. Neville started to ignore it since halftime was almost over, but he pulled the phone from his pocket anyway. He had no idea who the unknown number belonged to. He held up one finger, signaling Lexy that he needed a few moments.

"Is this Neville?" the woman on the other end of the phone asked.

"Yes, it is. Who's calling?"

"My name is Lakesha. I'm Lauren's friend. She asked me to call you and let you know that she got arrested and is in the county jail under a $35,000 bond."

Chapter 11

L auren walked into the small room that the correctional officer guided her to, and she saw a nicely dressed woman sitting at the small table with an expensive leather briefcase in front of her. The woman smelled like money. The cost of her briefcase and the woman's clothes combined was probably a few months' worth of rent for Lauren. She was so nervous that she trembled as she sat down while looking at the woman curiously. She had been in jail for three days, and Lauren had cried so much that her puffy eyes were almost swollen shut. She was sick with worry, and that had taken her appetite. But with how the food looked and smelled, she was glad she didn't want anything to eat. There was no way her body could digest the slop they served there. Just the smell of it the first day had made Lauren throw up.

She sat down and stared at the woman but didn't speak. Lauren hated jail, and she missed her son something terrible. As much as she hated jail, she was afraid to go home to nothing, so she wasn't sure she wanted to take the money she had left and post her bond. She would be free but wouldn't have the next month's rent or anything to fall back on. While in jail, she stood up and waited at the door to get the officer's attention several times so she could let her know that she'd talk. She'd give up Neville and tell Cedric everything he wanted to know, but something kept stopping her from doing so.

"My name is Emily Weinstein, and Neville hired me to be your attorney. He also gave me the money to post your bond, and the paperwork is being processed as we speak."

Lauren was so relieved that she couldn't stop the tears from falling. Mrs. Weinstein eyed her with an empathetic look. She'd had way more high-profile and interesting cases than this. Emily had defended people accused of murder, racketeering, drug trafficking, human trafficking, and even a case that involved a well-known madam and a brothel. This was almost beneath her, but Neville had paid her retainer, and he'd stroked her ego by calling her the best. She at least had to come and see what was happening, but in her professional opinion, Lauren should just give up Neville and continue with her life.

"How well do you know Neville?" Emily asked her.

"I don't know him well at all. We stayed at the same hotel for a couple of weeks, and then he left."

"You initially told the detective that you got the CPN number from a woman named Sarah. But the detectives have been looking for and building a case against Neville for this same exact crime. You said you don't know him well, so could you be afraid of him? You have a young son, correct? I'm just trying to put all of the pieces together. My go-to would be the fact that you do have a child and you have a clean record. I would try to push for house arrest or probation in cases like this, but they're going to play hardball because they want Neville. If you're against giving him up, that might end badly for you."

Lauren had no clue what she would do, but the fact that she was about to go home gave her a slight sense of relief. She had managed to get Lakesha to check her website and to call into her job for her. If her boss knew that she had been arrested for fraud, he might very well fire her, but now, she needed her job more than ever. Since Neville had come through and posted her bond, she didn't have to touch her money. For however long she remained free, she wanted to maintain the apartment she now had.

"How long do you think I can stay out before I would have to go to trial?"

"It depends. Once you bond out, your first court date will normally be thirty days or slightly less. I'm pretty sure I can get the case continued, and at that point, I can probably get a court date three to four months away from that date. I can't promise anything after that. To be on the safe side, I'd just say count on having your case heard no more than six months after today."

Lauren nodded. That should give her plenty of time to think and figure out what she wanted to do. She understood that people were confused about why she wouldn't give up Neville, but she stood on the fact that he didn't put a gun to her head and force her to use the CPN number. Lauren didn't want to do three years in prison, but he *had* changed her life for the better, even if it was only for a little bit. He could have left her high and dry, but he even came through and got her a lawyer and posted her bond. She had to consider that.

She was so happy to be going home that as soon as

Mrs. Weinstein stood up, her eyes filled with tears again. This had been the longest three days of her life. Then finally, it hit Lauren that if she could barely survive three days in jail, three years would be more than she could bear. So what was she going to do?

LAKESHA WATCHED HER FRIEND AND SHOOK HER HEAD AS Lauren drank the wine from her glass. She knew something was off about how fast her friend had gone from being virtually homeless to getting a fly-ass apartment and decking it out with all brand-new furniture.

As soon as Lauren had walked through the door, she went and took a shower, washed her hair, and brushed her teeth. She had just finished devouring a bacon, egg, and cheese sandwich when Assad ran through the door with Lakesha behind him. Lakesha wanted the tea bad as hell, but she wouldn't ask questions in front of Assad. She had told him that his mother had to go out of town for work. Assad had no clue that his mother was in jail, and he had been happy and content with Lakesha. She kept him busy and did fun things with him every day. Of course, Assad had fun with her, but as soon as he saw his mother, he ran into her arms.

It was tough for Lauren not to cry in front of her son, but she didn't want him to know anything was wrong. Lakesha waited patiently for an hour while Lauren talked to and played with Assad. He finally went into his room to watch YouTube on his iPad.

"Please, tell me how you ended up in fucking jail, Lauren."

Lauren stood up. "I need a refill on the wine. I've been through hell. I just want to get in bed and cuddle with my baby."

Lauren poured herself some more wine, then returned to the living room with Lakesha. She let out a big sigh before starting her story. She began with how Neville approached her and offered her a CPN number. Lakesha's eyes grew wide.

"I know quite a few people that have used those. I didn't know you could really go to jail for that."

"That's my point. It's not like I was out here committing hard-core crimes. This is some white-collar shit, but the detective who questioned me has it out for Neville. He said that he uses women and scams them. He wanted me to give up Neville."

Lakesha looked at her friend in awe. "And you did, right?"

She could tell from the look on Lauren's face that she hadn't. "Lauren," she stated in a hushed tone, "don't tell me you'd go to prison to protect this nigga. Bitch, he wouldn't do the same for you."

"All I know, Kesha, is that he didn't make me use the number. He gave me a choice. I knew it might come back to bite me in the ass, but I used it anyway and enjoyed every second of it. I was so grateful to get out of that funky-ass extended-stay hotel. I didn't see the side of Neville that the detective was talking about. Neville said he wanted to help Assad and me, and he did."

Lakesha shook her head. "I get it. I do. He didn't make you use the number, and you don't want to be labeled a snitch, but think about Assad. You'd lose your mind without him, and he would do the same without you. I would certainly take care of him while you were away, but it shouldn't come to that. Fuck Neville. You don't owe him a thing. You must put Assad first."

Her friend wasn't telling her anything that she didn't know. Lauren drank the rest of the wine in her glass, and she still had no buzz. Her emotions were all over the place, and she hated it. Giving up Neville seemed like the logical, commonsense thing to do, but she still wasn't sure. For the moment, Lauren just wanted to drop the subject.

"Has the studio had any bookings?"

"You used that CPN number to get that business too, didn't you?"

"I did, Lakesha. But does that even matter? I got it for a reason. I knew the CPN thing would run out eventually, and I wanted something to fall back on."

"As long as you remain free, I don't see you having an issue with that. That type of business is very popular now. It's also passive income and easy money. In the three days you were gone, you had more than six bookings and made $2,100."

Lauren breathed a sigh of relief. "That's not bad at all, and I'm going to work at the restaurant tomorrow. I just need some time to think about what to do, but while I'm at it, life must go on. I was reading up on the CPN shit, and I'm shocked that Cedric didn't freeze my bank accounts. So I will take out all of my money and use cash before he gets the bright idea to do so. After that, I think I'll be okay with what I have, the content studio, and the restaurant."

Lakesha wanted to say so much more, but she knew her friend had already been through a lot. Also, she didn't want to be the pot calling the kettle black. Her boyfriend wasn't a scammer, but he got his money by doing illegal things. She knew he would never intentionally put her in harm's way, but there was always a chance she would get jammed up if the police came for him. Her situation was different, though. She'd been with her man for years, and he'd held her down time and time again. He had done more for her than she could ever repay him for, and she still wasn't sure she'd protect him if the police ever wanted her to give him up. She knew how much Lauren loved her son, so this was odd to her.

"I hope you think long and hard when you're thinking about this. You know Assad will be good with me, but will that be good *for* him? He had already lost his father. I know you feel you owe this Neville character something, but you don't. He didn't make you use that number, but at the same time, his ass was already hot. He had the Feds on his ass, and that's why you got caught so quickly. You mean the world to that little boy in there. Think long and hard before you decide, Lauren. That's all I'm asking. I'll get going, so you can spend some time with Assad. Call me if you need anything."

Lauren stood so she could walk her friend to the door. "Thank you for everything. You really are the only person that I can count on. You've always been a good friend to me, Lakesha."

Lakesha blinked away tears as she hugged her friend. "We aren't crying today," she joked. "You don't have to thank me for being a good person. I love you."

Lakesha left her friend's apartment, praying that when the time came, she would do what she needed to do to save herself because if the tables were turned, she already knew that Neville wouldn't go down for Lauren.

Chapter 12

Lauren almost jumped out of her skin when she exited her job and ran into Cedric. Her heart raced with fear as she looked down at his hands. He didn't have cuffs out. Was he coming to arrest her again? Cedric could see the fear in Lauren's eyes, and that was precisely what he wanted. He wanted her to be afraid. "Lauren, I see you made your way back to work." He smiled at her while she looked over her shoulder.

The last thing she needed was for Carlos's nosy ass to know she had been arrested. "I have because I need the money. I handle credit and debit cards, and I might get fired if my boss finds out that I was arrested for identity theft and fraud." Her eyes were darting back and forth across his face. She was panicking.

"You're asking a lot for someone that refuses to cooperate with me. I shouldn't have to beg you to give me Neville, but I understand you may have some allegiance toward him. I also know that snitching isn't favorable among our people, so I can understand your hesitation.

However, I'm not blowing this case and letting Neville go for anyone. You have six days to decide what it is that you want to do, and if I still don't have Neville at the end of those six days, I will do anything and everything to make your life hell," Cedric promised before tipping his head in her direction and turning to walk away.

He stopped in his tracks and turned to look back at her. "Oh, and taking all the money from your accounts and maxing out the credit cards was smart."

He was on to her and about to start sticking it to her ass. Lauren stood frozen in place as she contemplated calling Neville but decided against it. What if her phone was tapped? She looked down at the device in her hand as if it were a snake.

"Fuck," she hissed as she walked toward her car.

Every day she was getting deposits and bookings for her content studio, which was the easiest money she had ever made. People wanted to use the studio for social media content, maternity photoshoots, birthday shoots, marketing and branding shoots, etc. Lauren had even thought about adding some cute and fun décor and themes and having a section that was a selfie museum. People could come in and take selfies and photos in the museum and post fun, creative pictures on social media. Everything was about social media these days, and Lauren intended to capitalize off it . . . but for how long?

If she didn't give up Neville, she might only be free for six months. Lauren couldn't believe that it was even a decision for her to make. She loved Assad with every fiber of her being and didn't want to leave him. Tears streamed down her cheeks as she drove toward the school to pick him up. She had made up her mind. In the next six days, she had to tell Cedric everything he wanted to know about Neville.

NEVILLE SAT WATCHING HIS LAWYER, EMILY, INTENSELY. She was Jewish and one of the best lawyers in the area. She looked up from the paper she'd been reading and stared him directly in the eyes.

"I will be very honest with you, Mr. James. It's not looking good for Lauren, and if she is found guilty at trial, her son Assad will go into foster care. According to the documents before me, his father is deceased, and she has no relationships with his family. I'm showing one sibling, but he has an extensive record, and even though he's family, the child won't be placed with him if he doesn't have a job or a stable living environment. The DA is out for blood, and deals aren't on the table. Especially because who they really want is you. If she doesn't give you up, they won't have any mercy on her, and from what I can gather, she won't talk because you're sitting here in front of me."

Neville matched the lawyer's intense stare. The wheels in his head were turning, but he remained cool on the outside. Finally, with a nod of his head, he stood up. "I reached out to you because you're one of the best lawyers in Charlotte and the surrounding areas. Just keep doing what you do; hopefully, things will work out without anyone having to do any time."

Neville turned to leave before he could take in the doubtful look in her eyes. Emily Weinstein was a beast in the courtroom, but she wasn't a miracle worker. She was very intelligent, on top of her game, and had connections. Even still, she had to choose her battles. She couldn't grease palms, offer bribes, and call in favors for every single case that she worked. Her track record was impeccable; even still, she'd suffered losses in her thirteen-year career. Neville had the money necessary to retain her, but he wasn't a high-profile client, nor was his case one for which she could charge dozens of billable hours. This case wasn't a cash cow for her, and she wasn't sure it would be worth the risk of sticking her neck out for this Lauren woman, even if she were a single mother. Emily wanted to know why this woman refused to give him up. What was it about Neville? Was she afraid of him? Surely, she couldn't be that indebted to him that she'd risk jail time and losing her only son to the system to protect him.

Neville walked out of the large building that housed Emily's office and hit the unlock button on the key fob to his Porsche truck. Inside, he looked at the items sprawled out on his passenger seat. His passport and a boarding pass to Bali were his tickets to freedom. It was all he needed to escape and lie low from the FBI. Once he was home free, he could clear his mind, and thoughts of Lauren and Assad would be pushed out of his head. Neville was the kind of man who only cared about himself. People were disposable, especially once he got what he wanted out of them. And Lauren was no different.

At least, that's what he kept trying to tell himself. Neville didn't understand why he had this nagging desire to help her. It was, after all, his fault that she got jammed up. And she was going out of her way not to give him up, even though it might mean losing Assad. The thought of the bright-eyed, intelligent, mild-mannered child in foster care made his blood run cold. The chances were too great that he'd end up with a family that didn't give half a fuck about him and only wanted him around for the check. But that wasn't really his problem.

Neville sighed and looked at his diamond-encrusted Rolex. He had two hours before his plane took off toward Bali. After some contemplating, Neville started his truck. Fuck it. He had tried to show Lauren a better way, and he hated that she'd gotten jammed up, but it wasn't his concern. He had his ticket to freedom and couldn't see himself not using it.

Chapter 13

Lauren left her job with aching feet. Even though she still had access to a nice amount of money, she still couldn't stop working. At the moment, she had Lakesha at the content studio while it was being used. Lauren was confident that if her bookings remained consistent for another few weeks, she could leave the restaurant and not look back. She had also been brainstorming other business ideas because one just wasn't enough. Lauren had contemplated everything from making candles and body butter to signing up for classes so she could learn to be a masseuse. For once, the possibilities felt endless. She wanted to work just as hard for herself as she had slaving at the restaurant, and she knew the reward would be greater.

"Excuse me, Lauren?" a woman walked up to her, uncertain whether she had the right person.

Lauren eyed the pretty woman. "Yes?" She had never seen her before and wanted to know how the woman knew her name.

"Hi. My name is Tomica, and I was just wondering if I could have a moment of your time."

"About?"

Tomica blew out a deep breath like what she was about to say would require a lot of strength. "Cedric, well, Detective Johnson, is my brother. He's working this case because he's in law enforcement but also because it's close to his heart. I'm the person that Neville scammed and took advantage of."

Lauren shook her head, confused. "Wait, so your brother thinks it's professional and okay to tell my business? How is that even safe for me that a complete stranger knows where I live, what I look like, and where I work? Is this considered witness tampering because it sounds very much illegal?" She didn't like the idea of anyone tracking her down to convince her to snitch on Neville.

"Please don't look at it like that. I'm a victim, and he's just keeping me up to date on what's going on with the case. He was so happy when he finally thought he had Neville, but you won't cooperate for whatever reason, and he might get away. I can't tell you what to do, but I doubt you deserve to be in prison more than Neville. He's a rotten-ass person and a selfish human being. He uses his good looks and charm to manipulate and rob women blind. He's too lazy to get a real job, so he's just content with being a professional scammer. He drives around in exotic cars, wears designer clothes, and eats at fancy restaurants like that's really his life. Neville is a fake and a fraud. I'm not the only woman that he's done this to. So don't go down for him. Let him get the punishment he deserves."

Tomica was almost begging. Now, months later, she still hated the day she met Neville's charming ass. He had talked her out of more than just her panties, which ruined her life. Tomica still wasn't back to where she was financially or mentally before she met Neville, and she wasn't sure she would be anytime soon.

"I'm very sorry that this happened to you. I've been hearing bad things about Neville from different people, and while I don't doubt what you all say is true, I have never seen that side of him. I had to weigh the pros and cons of everything and decide for myself what I would do. Respectfully, I ask that you let the decision be mine. I have a lot to deal with and think about."

That wasn't what Tomica wanted to hear, but she would drop it . . . for now. According to her brother, quite a few women had come forth and were willing to testify against Neville. If he ever made it to those handcuffs, she did not doubt that he would be prosecuted to the fullest extent of the law. She'd make sure she never missed a day of the trial and would sing like a bird, telling everything she knew. Tomica gave a tight smile and walked away from Lauren. She could only hope and pray that Lauren would come to her senses. A man like Neville didn't deserve to be protected.

Inside her car, Lauren exhaled a deep breath. She had been prolonging the inevitable, but she just needed to go ahead and get it over with. She looked at her watch and saw that she had a few more hours before she had to pick up Assad from school. She had taken the early shift at work to get off early in the day. The entire time that she drove, Lauren's hands were trembling. She finally had to grip the steering wheel firmly and squeeze it until her knuckles almost turned white for them to stop shaking.

Lauren ended up at Ms. Weinstein's office. Since she didn't have an appointment, she was directed to the waiting room, where she sat still, trembling for almost fifteen minutes before Amy came and got her.

"Hi, Lauren. This is a surprise. We can head to my office, and you can tell me what I can do for you."

Lauren's heart drummed loudly as she followed Amy down a long hall. They finally reached her office, and she stood back and let Lauren enter first. Amy walked over to her desk and took a seat. "What brings you in today?"

Lauren wiped her sweaty hands down the legs of her jeans. "I, um, I want to cooperate. I didn't get the CPN number from a woman named Sarah. I got it from Neville. I don't know where he lives or anything about him other than his first name and his telephone number," she admitted truthfully. "Do you still think you could get me off with house arrest or probation?" she asked fearfully.

The shock was wearing off, and it was hitting Lauren that she really might have to leave Assad and go to jail. She wasn't even sure why she still had her apartment or the money from the scam, but she was grateful. Lauren was trying to give her son a better life, but she'd never use illegal means to do so ever again.

"I can take all that you said and use it when it's your time to go to court, but Neville turned himself in about an hour ago. He requested that you be granted full immunity, and I am waiting to hear back on whether those terms will be accepted."

Chapter 14

Neville sat with his back against the wall staring at his cell door. He had been in jail for three days and was still unsure if he would bother with posting bond. He knew he might as well get it over with, and the longer he sat in the county, whatever he got sentenced with, he could only hope they'd allow his time in jail to count as time served. Then suddenly, Neville's door opened, and one of the COs stood at his door and jerked his head.

"Let's go. You have a visitor."

Neville wanted to ask questions, but he didn't. It had to be Amy because who else would come to visit him? Neville didn't deal with many. He had very little family and even fewer friends. The women he came up off of were the ones he occupied most of his free time with, and since he had been outed for being a scammer, he knew none of them were coming within ten feet of him unless it was to bring him harm. Neville hadn't made anyone aware that he would turn himself in because he didn't think anyone cared.

Full of questions, he stood up and walked to the door to be handcuffed. After the handcuffs were placed on his hands in front of him, the CO led Neville to the visitation room. Despite his unfortunate circumstances, he was still a man; his eyes zeroed in on her round, plump ass. Just the thought of him not being able to have sex for the next however many years was enough to depress the hell out of him. He could have been in Bali out on the beach getting drunk and enjoying life, but he had to go and develop a soft spot for a woman he barely knew and her kid.

No one could tell Neville that Lauren didn't love Assad. So even he was baffled when Amy told him more than once that Lauren refused to talk. That tugged at his heartstrings more than he ever wanted to admit, and he just didn't understand why he had such a soft spot for Assad. He finally reasoned that maybe if more adults had cared and had soft spots for him, his life wouldn't have turned out the way it did. Neville had slept in some savage places. He wasn't sure if any of them were as savage as a prison, but the lifestyle he'd grown accustomed to after he started scamming wasn't how he grew up. Neville knew he could survive in prison. He could survive anywhere. However, the prison wasn't a place for a woman like Lauren, and foster care wasn't a place for a kid like Assad.

When Neville arrived in the visitation room, he was surprised to see Lauren. Very surprised. She looked beautiful as always. She had braids in her hair, and they made her look youthful and vibrant. The longer he stared into her face, the more he had to admit that Lauren was bad as hell. Without all of the additives and extra shit, she was gorgeous in a Nia Long and Halle Berry back in the '90s type of way. She didn't have to do the most to be considered gorgeous. Neville sat down and peeped that Lauren looked nervous.

"I didn't expect to see you here. What's going on? Is everything okay?" he asked, and he appeared genuinely concerned.

"I think I should be asking you that. You're the one in jail. I hate that you had to come here, but I wanted to look you in the face and tell you that I finally cracked. I gave Amy what I knew, which isn't much, but she will try to argue it so that I can get off without jail time."

Neville offered a small smile. "I appreciate that, but I wouldn't expect anything less. You don't owe me anything, Lauren. I was doing this CPN shit way before I knew you, and the CPN thing isn't the major thing. I'm into a few other things that go much deeper than that."

"Yeah. I've heard a few stories about how you're a not-so-great guy." Neville saw the flicker of disappointment in her eyes.

"I won't deny that. I'm actually not. I don't want it to sound like I'm making excuses, so I hesitate to explain myself, but I just come from nothing. And when I say nothing, I don't mean just material things. I don't have a lot of family or friends to care about me. Nobody was out here praying for me or wishing me well, and it gave me a real care-about-nobody-but-myself-fuck-it attitude. It's been that way for as long as I can remember, so in my mind, when I was looking out for myself and making sure I was good, I couldn't stop to worry about who would be feeling like this or that when it was all said and done."

"But it is in you to care about someone. You're not a

monster, Neville. Look at what you did for Assad and me. It was illegal, but it changed my life, and I don't even know if I regret it. Assad loves his new home, his new room, and the friends he has in the neighborhood. You did that for my baby and me. All we ever encountered at the extended stay were poor elderly people, pimps, prostitutes, and drug addicts."

"I did one good deed. I don't think that makes me a good person or even capable of being a good person. We all have weak moments. I guess you and Assad just made me have one. It was about time I did some good in life, so I just chalked it up to that."

"You can deny it all you want to, but I still say you're a good person. You have it in you, and Assad still asks about you."

"Tell Li'l Man I said what's up. Tell him to stay out of trouble."

"Will do. I put some money on your books too. I hope $200 is enough."

Neville was pleasantly surprised. He hadn't expected Lauren to do anything for him. He was amazed that she didn't hate him. "I can definitely do something with that, but you don't have to spend your money on me."

"It's the least I can do. You said you don't really have anyone that cares about you, and that's not true. I care, and I'm here."

Neville dropped his head and shook it. The last thing he needed was for her to become attached to him and to have some kind of hope for him or them. "I don't know what you want to see in me so badly, but I'm not that guy. I do appreciate the gesture, however."

Neville never depended on or counted on anyone while

he was on the streets, so he for damn sure wasn't going to get used to the idea of Lauren visiting him and keeping money on his books. On the other hand, Neville was more than prepared to do his time alone. She didn't have to explain anything to him, and she didn't have to do anything for him. All he needed her to do was keep caring for Assad and not fail him as a mother. Assad had a better chance of growing up to be a standup guy with a mother like Lauren raising him. There was no telling how he could turn out if he got lost in the system.

The visit ended, and Lauren gave Neville a small smile. "I'll keep you in my prayers."

Neville smiled back and nodded at her. "Baby, God forgot about me a long time ago, but you do that. Who knows. Maybe he'll listen to you."

Lauren was green as hell but in a good way. No matter what she'd been through, she didn't let it harden her or make her bitter, and he could appreciate that about her. She even took the money she should have saved and put it on his books. As he was led back to his cell, Neville thought he didn't regret helping her at all. It actually felt pretty dope to do a good deed.

Chapter 15

Neville sat in the rec room with his arms folded and his eyes trained on the television in the front of the room. He was watching a football game like he did on most Sundays during the season. He no longer got courtside seats to NBA games or sat in the bleachers for NFL games. Neville had done four months in the county jail before being sentenced to three years in prison. Considering what he could have gotten, that was a slap on the wrist. Five years was actually the maximum, but Amy was confident that he could be out in three with good behavior and the time he had already served. A CO entered the room and said something to the officer standing there.

"James!" His name was yelled, and Neville looked away from the television.

"You have a visitor. Let's go!"

Officer Ham was one of the few female correctional officers that gave him a hard time. She wasn't easy on the eyes at all, and she was built like a linebacker. Out in the world, men that looked like Neville never gave her a second look or the time of day. It had been the popular, handsome guys that made her life hell in school and college. At thirty, she'd only had two boyfriends in her life. Not even guys that were considered ugly paid her any mind most days. Her anger, bitterness, and low self-esteem caused her to come to work and be a bitch most days. Her job allowed her to give men a hard time, and she enjoyed it. On occasion, she'd get her feelings hurt by an ill-tempered inmate that would cuss her out and call her every derogatory name under the sun.

One day, she left work in tears, but that didn't stop her from returning to work and continuing her terror. When inmates made her mad, she'd purposely withhold their mail, write them up for any little thing, and cause them to lose their privileges. She tried that tough shit with Neville, but he ignored her dumb ass.

Neville stood up and followed her to the visitation room, eyeing her broad back and square-shaped ass the entire way. When he entered the room, his eyes did a quick scan, and it didn't take him long to spot Lauren. He hadn't seen her in four months, but she was still as fine as ever, and even with her sitting down, he could tell she looked like money. Her shoulder-length hair was in loose curls, and she had lash extensions that brought out her light-colored eyes. Her nails were done, and he could tell from her top half that she wore a wrap dress. It was purple, and the color looked radiant against her skin.

She stood up when he neared the table, and Neville hugged her. He hadn't seen or spoken to her, but she put money on his books weekly. She was the one who had been keeping him afloat during this bid.

"Don't think I'm an asshole," Neville stated as he sat down. "I didn't have your number memorized, and I didn't have your address memorized either. So that's why I haven't called or written you, but I want to thank you for keeping money on my books."

"It's the least I can do after you posted my bond and hired a lawyer for me. It's just me returning the favor. How have you been?"

"I'm alive. That's the best answer I can give. What about you? You damn sure look good."

Lauren smiled wide. "Thank you. I feel good too. I had court Thursday, and I got four years' probation. And last month, I made the most money I've ever made with my content studio. I've been booked out of the ass. Last week, I made in one week what it took me two months to make when I first started. It's insane how many photographers don't have their own studio, so they mostly do shoots outside or against plain backdrops.

"Now that I have a space they can rent, I have certain photographers that book with me weekly, and they'll rent the space out for six or seven hours at a time. I've made $1,050 off one particular photographer the last four days. He doesn't mind paying me $150 per hour when his clients pay him $400 and up for their shoots. Lowkey, I need to get into photography. He charges like $500 for maternity photoshoots."

Neville smiled as Lauren talked a mile a minute. "I'm happy for you. How is Li'l Man?"

Lauren beamed with pride. "He is doing awesome. He just started playing flag football, and he's having a ball with that. You should see him with his little self running on that field. I love him so much."

"I love to hear that. Damn, I wish I could see him, but I'd never ask you to bring him to a place like this. Just tell him not to forget me."

"I won't. So, there's something I need to tell you." Lauren went from smiling hard and looking happy to suddenly looking nervous.

"What is it?" he asked curiously.

"It's kind of hard to tell in this dress, and I stood back when I hugged you, so I'm sure you didn't feel it, but, um, I'm pregnant. I'm carrying small, but I'm five months."

Neville's brows shot up. He didn't even have to calculate too hard to know that it was roughly five months ago when they had sex.

"I'm not sure if the condom broke or what, but I can assure you that I haven't had sex with anyone else besides you."

Neville was stunned. He never wanted kids. He never thought about having kids. This was a shock to his system, and on top of that, he'd be incarcerated for the next three years. But he didn't really have a say in the matter because it was too late for her to have an abortion, so he could only assume she wanted the child.

"I didn't expect that." Neville didn't know what else to say.

"Being a single mother is one of the hardest things I've ever done, but I couldn't bring myself to get an abortion. On top of it being the hardest thing I've ever done, it's also the most rewarding. The content studio is thriving, and I also learned how to make candles. I don't make as much money from it as I do with the content studio, but I profit around $1,000 a month, and I can only pray that it continues to grow.

"On top of that, I've been able to clean up my credit, and I can now use my own Social Security number and get approved for things. Life is so different for me than how it was before with Assad. So I think I can give this baby a good life. And if it's not what you want, I can totally respect that."

Neville had tried so hard to fight it, especially when he knew he was no good for Lauren, but she refused to see the bad in him. Having someone in his corner was new for him, but he couldn't keep running from it. Not when she was sitting right across from him, telling him she was carrying his child. Neville reached over the table and grabbed Lauren's hand.

"I have to be honest with you. I've never wanted to love anyone because they either hurt you or leave you or both. Hell, I don't even really know what love is, especially from a man to a woman. I've never experienced it or seen it, but my mother told me when you rather the hurt come to you than them, that's how I would know. I'm not perfect, and I don't even know if I'm worthy of being loved by you or anyone. But I know I'd rather sit inside this hellhole than know you were here and I was away from Assad. Lauren, we can give this baby and Assad a good life if you allow me."

Epilogue

Lauren gathered her things, including a small diaper bag with her baby's milk, diapers, snacks, and coloring books for Assad. Usually, she would not be able to carry a bag into the prison at all, but she had gotten permission since the baby was only three months old. However, the staff checked every nook and cranny of the bag and all its contents.

As they walked toward the prison entrance, she couldn't help but feel anxious. It had been months since she last visited Neville, and she knew he must be looking forward to seeing them. This would be the first time Neville saw the baby since she gave birth.

"Mommy, why do we have to come here?" asked Assad.

"Remember, sweetie, we talked about it. We're coming to see Neville. He hasn't met the baby yet, and he's been waiting," Lauren explained, holding his hand as they walked down the corridor.

"But why do we have to come here? Why come he can't just come home?"

"It's 'why' Assad, not 'why come,'" Lauren corrected him. "And Neville can't come home right now because he made a mistake and did something bad. He has to stay here for a while until he can come home, but we can visit him. It's important that we show him that we love him and support him."

Assad nodded, his eyes wide as they entered the visitor's area. They were led to a small room with a table and chairs, where Neville was already waiting for them.

Lauren smiled as she looked at her man. Even though he was incarcerated, he looked damn good.

"Lauren, Assad! Hey! I've missed you both so much," Neville exclaimed, a huge smile on his face.

Assad ran toward Neville, hugging him tightly. "Hi, Neville! Guess what? I'm a big brother! Mommy had a baby."

Neville's eyes widened with happiness as he hugged Assad back and winked at Lauren. "I know. I bet you're the best big brother, huh?"

"Uh-huh." Assad nodded happily, sitting next to Neville, taking his coloring book from the bag, and immediately started coloring. "But she cries a lot."

"She?" Neville asked, looking at Lauren cradling a small bundle.

"Yes. She," Lauren smiled. "Meet your daughter, Mia."

Lauren turned the baby toward Neville, and he instantly felt a lump in his throat. He stared at the baby and could already see so much of him in her.

"A girl," he whispered, taking her little hand. "Wow."

Neville's heart swelled with pride, and a small part of him felt like he was getting his Karma. He had caused so many women pain, and now, here he was, a father to a little girl.

"She's beautiful," he admired.

Mia gripped his finger with her tiny hand, and Neville choked back tears.

"Is everything okay with her?" he questioned. "There weren't any complications or anything, huh?"

"No," Lauren smiled. "Mia was born a happy and healthy baby girl." She sat down in the chair, and Assad sat next to her.

Neville's face grew serious. "Lauren, I know I messed up. I'm sorry for the pain I've caused you and our family. I promise I'll do better once I get out of here."

Lauren nodded, grateful for the apology. "I know you will, Neville. I know I'm not 100 percent to blame, but I also know that you might not be here now if it hadn't been for me."

Neville frowned at what he heard and watched her get comfortable with the baby. "Don't even say anything like that, Lauren. Look, I got me in here. Even if I hadn't helped you, I would've ended up in here eventually. So don't do that."

Lauren nodded, not knowing what to say.

"Can I hold her?" Neville motioned toward Mia.

"Of course," she smiled, gently handing him the baby. Her heart swelled watching Neville holding his daughter.

Neville stared at his beautiful baby and could feel a lump forming in his throat again. "She's so beautiful," he whispered.

Lauren smiled and looked between Assad, busy coloring, and Neville holding Mia. Despite the situation, she felt extremely happy. She had come a long way from the

Extended Stay. She locked eyes with Neville, and he flashed his signature smile, warming her heart.

"What?" she asked.

"I'm just . . . grateful," he said. "I can't wait to get home and wake up to you every day . . . to change my baby girl's diapers in the middle of the night."

"Hey, what about me?" Assad piped up, looking up at Neville.

Neville smiled, shifting the baby slightly. "We can play all the video games you want."

Assad beamed and started dancing in his seat, causing Lauren to laugh. "Can we still talk on the phone until you come home?"

"Of course," he assured him. "Assad, I promise you, I'll be the best father I can be. I'll always be there for you, no matter what." Neville kissed the top of his head and hugged him with his free arm.

Assad returned the hug to him tightly. "I love you, Neville," he said.

"I love you too, Li'l Man." Neville looked up at Lauren and smiled. "I'll be home soon, and I'll never leave either of your sides," he promised.

Lauren smiled at Neville and leaned in for a kiss. "You are going to be a wonderful father."

Neville replied, "Thank you for changing me."

Lauren looked at him quizzically. "I didn't change you; love did," she said.

Neville smiled, feeling grateful for the love that he had in his life. He hugged Lauren and Assad close to him, cherishing the moment. Then kissing his baby girl, he knew that they would always be there for each other no matter their challenges.

The End

TEARS IN THE TRAP SNIPPET

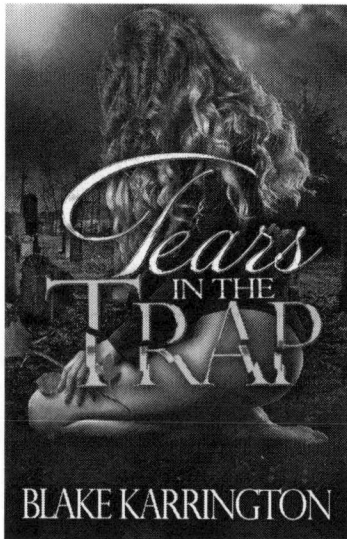

PROLOGUE

My name is Tiffany "Baby Girl" Scott, and as I stand here today, I have come to regret the fact that I killed him. Yes, I said it. I killed a man, and for reason's I thought was justifiable. From as far back as I can remember, I have been lied to, manipulated, verbally and physically abused at the hands of the person who I thought was supposed to protect me. I been through it all and I can still taste the blood in my mouth from when my mother, Camille, knocked me clean across the room because I forgot to do the dishes. I been burnt with a skillet, dragged around by my hair and almost drowned twice in the bath tub. My mother had pure evil in her heart for me.

Those were the days, days that are dead and gone. I'm 18 now and she probably fears me more than the devil himself. At the end of it all, she, along with my father made me the cold hearted person I am today. It was my mother who told me that I wasn't going to amount to anything. It was my mother who blamed me for something that I had no control over. It was my mother who hated me because I was the product of a rape. How could I be responsible for something my biological father did?

I guess you can say that my situation is a little complicated, but for the record, I never meant for any of this to transpire the way that it did. I wish that things were different. I wish that my mother cared and loved me enough to tell me the truth about everything from the very beginning. I wish I knew what I know now, but it's too late. The damage is done and I have to live with the consequences of my actions. Actions that may end up making me the next person to meet the angel of death. Let me take you back, and show you how this whole ordeal unfolded and placed me at this point of life and death. I'm Baby Girl, and this is my unfinished story.

CHAPTER ONE

"So are you going to Prom or what, and don't gimme that shit that you don't have a date either."

Tiffany didn't hear a word her best friend Jayden had spoken. At that moment all her attention was focused on Nasir who was being dropped off at school by his dad. Every time Hassan brought Nasir to school it was like a car show. One day it was a BMW and the next a Range Rover. One week Hassan switched cars for every day, he wanted to make sure his son enjoyed all the benefits of being his boy. He remembered what his high school life was like and made sure that Nasir's was in every way what he had always wished for.

Baby Girl," Jayden yelled, snapping her finger in front of Tiffany's face to get her out of her daze.

"I told you girl, for the tenth time, I'm not going," Tiffany replied, waving Jayden off. Her friend had been bothering her the whole weekend about her decision to not attend their senior prom. Tiffany didn't want to let

Jayden know the reason, because she knew her friend would try to convince her to go anyway.

Before Tiffany could go into her made up excuses, Nasir walked up on her, flashing his tantalizing smile.

"Wassup baby Girl. Wassup Jayden," he spoke, while tapping Tiffany on the arm.

"Hey Nasir".

When it came to Nasir, Tiffany was all the way open and would do anything for him. Not only was he handsome and had a nice body, Nasir was also the captain of the basketball team and Tiffany's boyfriend. He had college recruiters coming to every one of his basketball games. It was said that The University of Kentucky was even hoping, that he brought his talents to their school.

"Tiff I need to holla at you about something," Nasir announced, lightly pulling her away from Jayden.

"Ta hell wit y'all too," Jayden smiled, rolling her eyes and heading for her first period class.

"I was wondering if you wanted to go to the prom. I know I told you that I wasn't going to be able to go, but the dates for the SAT's has changed and I really want to attend it with my main girl...

"Yea I'll go," Tiffany said, cutting him off, while trying to not show her excitement.

She really had no plans on attending after Nasir had shot her down the first time, but as long as he was now with it, her excitement had returned. Tiffany was a nice piece and outside of her average dressing attire, she was definitely one of the hottest girls in the school. Golden Bronze skin, cute face, long black hair and a set of slanted almond-shaped eyes that would draw anyone in. Outside of a long scar on her neck from when her cousin tried to cut her throat, Tiffany was flawless. With Nasir being the hottest guy in school, it was only right that he snatched her up.

"Aight, I'll text you later so we can hit the mall up. Don't worry about ya wardrobe, it's on me," Nasir concluded. He knew Tiffany's financial situation and would never put that burden on her, especially knowing that his family had more than enough to cover everything.

He looked around the school halls and was tempted to still a kiss but the principle and a few teachers gathered together made him decide not to. Instead he just flashed his smile and with a wink of his eye headed towards his class.

HASSAN GRABBED HIS PHONE AND SCROLLED THROUGH IT as he headed down Plaza Road. At the young age of 38, he was still in the dope game and had the streets of Charlotte on lock down. If heroin was sold anywhere in the city, more than likely it came from him, and if you wasn't a part of his team, you certainly wish you were. Everybody was making money, all the way down to the look outs. That was also the reason why he had some of the city's most feared stick-up boys always on his mind, and from the looks of today, they were at work.

"You muthafucka's think that I'm slippin," Hassan mumbled to himself, looking in his rearview mirror at the black Impala that had been following him around all morning.

He ruled out the possibility that it was the police, a few miles back, considering that the tail was so sloppy. A better look at the driver of the Impala when they both pulled up to a red light, certainly confirmed his suspicions. It was rare that you would see two black cops riding around together and Hassan noticed what appeared to be the barrel of a large caliber assault rifle.

"I dare one of you niggas to make a move," Hassan threaten, as if they could hear him. He gently reached in-between his seat and grabbed a hold to his 17 shot Beretta.

He had a little more than 100k in the car and was going to protect it, and his life, by any means necessary. Hassan could see the blitz coming like a NFL quarterback, and sure enough, right before the light turned green, the passenger and the driver of the Impala jumped out of the car. Seeing that they both had guns in their hands, he didn't hold back and began to let the bullets fly. Pop, Pop, Pop, Pop!

All four shots, blasted through Hassan's car window and right into the direction of the would-be stick-up boys. They both immediately took cover, but not before letting off a few shots at Hassan who had peeled off through the red light. The gunman jumped back into the Impala and punched it through the crossroads as well. They didn't get far because the heavy traffic at the intersection prevented them from doing so. They would have been the cause of a major accident if it wasn't for the quick thinking of the Impala's driver slamming on breaks.

Hassan dipped in and out of traffic, holding the steering wheel with one hand and clutching the gun in the other. His adrenaline was pumping and it wasn't until he looked back up into his mirror that he realized that the Impala wasn't behind him. He began to slow down, and everything seemed to be alright, that was until Hassan felt a burning sensation coming from his shoulder. He gazed down and saw that the whole side of his yellow Polo T-shirt was covered with blood. That's when he knew he had been shot.

It was the usual when Tiffany arrived home from school. Her mom was stretched out on the couch in her old torn robe with mix-matched panties and bra, looking a hot mess. Tiffany stood over top of her, looking down at Camil in disgust. Cocaine residue was all over the coffee table, along with an empty bottle of Gin and three empty Corona bottles. At one point in time, Tiffany could remember when her mom had it going on. For a thick woman, Camil was a head-turner back in the day, and she made it hard for most men to resist her. Camil was definitely the reason why Tiffany had such curves. Even now, when she wanted to Camil could clean up very nicely. But that was something she hadn't done in nearly six years. Tiffany always felt like she was the one to blame, and not because she really was, but because Camil always told her it was all her fault that Mark had left. Mark was Camil's fiancé and boyfriend for over four years. They had planned to be married that summer but his inability to keep his hands off a young Tiffany had derailed the wedding. Tiffany really liked Mark at first, he was the father she never had and Mark seemed to want to fulfill the role. But once Tiffany began to fill out and puberty hit, Mark's intentions began to change. He started insisting that Camil give him and Tiffany alone time for them to bond. Camil thought it was strange but was so in love with Mark that she allowed it. In her mind it was no way the man she was about to marry could be interested in an eleven-year-old. For a young Tiffany things went from small request to come sit on his lap, to him being in the bathroom when she got out the shower. He would force her to dry off in front of him. Still Tiffany was unaware of what had changed between her and Mark's relationship. Mark had always been so nice to her often bringing her gifts and taking her to get ice cream, her favorite dessert. But all that changed on March 2nd of that year. Tiffany would never forget the look in Mark's eye after he turned towards her from watching Camil leave from the window.

"Did you have a good day at school today?" Mark asked Tiffany as he shifted his gaze back toward the window. With the taillights of Camil's car no longer visible, he knew he only had a small timeframe to do what he'd been wanting to do for the last few weeks.

Tiffany embarrassingly dropped her head and used her small fingers to play with the hem of her pink jean skirt. "I guess it was ok."

"So why the long face?" Mark asked as he moved to sit on the couch in the living room.

His eyes lustfully roamed over Tiffany's young body as he licked his lips and adjusted himself. Her skirt was mid-thigh and kind of short showing off her thick thighs and legs while the colorful stripped shirt she had on hugged her curves and small breast like a glove. To only be eleven, Tiffany was filling out in all the right places which was a bad thing for her, especially with men like Mark around. Looking at her face, you could tell she was young, but looking at her body, you'd think she was in her late teens. Camil noticed the fast rate her daughter had started to develop, but thought nothing of it since she blossomed at a young age herself.

"It's nothing." Tiffany responded walking further into the living room.

Mark laughed. "I can tell it's something by the look on your face." He smiled at her. "What really happened at school today Tiffany? You know you can tell me anything, right?"

At that moment, Tiffany lifted her head high and held his gaze. Although some of the things Mark made her do whenever Camil left the house or was too drugged up to notice what was going on had her a little confused, she still trusted him to be that father figure she was missing in her life.

"Well...today at recess when we were playing tag, Bobby Jones touched my butt then kissed me on the cheek." She replied blushing. When Tiffany didn't hear a response from Mark, she looked over at him on the couch and smiled, only to be met with a weird curl of his full lips and a blank stare.

If Tiffany's mind was as mature as her body, she would've noticed the change in Mark's demeanor behind the fake smile. A flash of anger crossed his face, while his body went stiff and his jaw tightened at the thought of someone else touching his precious baby girl. Mark didn't know where this obsession with his fiancé's daughter came from, but he wasn't going to tolerate anyone getting close to what he claimed in his demented mind to already belong to him. Biting his bottom lip until he almost punctured a small gash in it, he regained control over his temper and continued to give Tiffany his undivided attention.

"How did you feel when this little jerk Bobby touched your butt?" He asked through tight lips.

Tiffany smiled again and shrugged her shoulders. "I don't know. I guess I liked it since I like him. I mean...when you like a boy, aren't you suppose to let him kiss and touch you?"

Mark slowly nodded his head. "Yeah, it can mean that. Perfect example is the way we touch each other because I like you and you like me." He patted the seat next to him for Tiffany to come sit down. For a second she hesitated because she knew what her sitting so close to him would lead up to. Yeah, Tiffany liked Mark, maybe even loved him, but not in the way he seemed to be convinced of.

As soon as Tiffany sat down, Mark's hand instantly went to her exposed thigh. With his thumb brushing against her soft skin, he drew imaginary circles back and forth. His breath became rigid and his eyes dropped real low.

"You do know that I like you too don't you Baby Girl?"

She nodded her head but remained silent. So many things started to circulate through Tiffany's mind just to keep her from freaking out. Mark's touches to her had always been weird in the past but for some reason, his touch today seemed different. The look in his eyes was even different. Tiffany could feel Mark looking at her, but kept her vision on anything but him at that moment. When she tried to put a little space between the two, he gripped her thigh to stop her from moving.

"Where you going?" Mark asked, eyes never leaving the sight of her plum-sized breast.

"I...I...I was going to get the remote to turn on the TV." Tiffany stammered with her words, something she did whenever she became real nervous. "I think *The Wiz* is on right now."

Without another word, she leaned over and grabbed the remote from off of the coffee table. A low groan escaped from Marks throat when her breast landed on top of his over turned hand.

"Is it ok that I watch it? Mark nodded his head. "Do you like this movie too?" He nodded his head again and moved his hand further up Tiffany's thigh. She swallowed the small lump in her throat and with shaky hands began pressing the channel button up, flipping through the channels until it landed on the station playing The Wiz. She smiled at her favorite part of the movie that was about to come up.

"This is almost the end of the movie. What you smiling for?"

"It's my favorite part." She said with her smile reaching her eyes. "I love when Diana Ross sings the last song." Tiffany looked up at Mark expecting him to be sharing in the same excitement she was for watching one of her favorite movies, but all she saw when she looked in his face, was a predatory look in his eyes and a smirk playing across his lips.

"You know, your mom is going to be gone for a minute. How about you show me how much you like me while your favorite part plays on the TV."

Tiffany's little body went stiff at Mark's words. She never did like the little games he would teach her whenever her mom was gone and this time was no different, regardless of what was playing on TV. When she tried to voice her concerns to Mark though, he wasn't trying to hear it.

"Oh, so you can let that little nigga touch on your butt and kiss on you, but I can't?" He asked, attitude laced all over his tone. "If anything, I should be the only nigga touching and kissing you."

When Tiffany didn't respond to anything he'd just said, Mark turned to her with a menacing stare as if he just realized something by her silence. "You letting this little nigga touch my pussy too?"

Tiffany tried to speak, but she was too scared to say a word. Mark had always gotten a little crazy whenever they talked about the boys at her school, but never like this. Tiffany prayed that whatever her mom was doing right now would just stop and she'd be on her way home. She even prayed that her real father would come busting through the door to save her from whatever games Mark had in store. But like all of the other times before, her prayers went unanswered and she was left to deal with him and his perverted ways.

"Well since you can't answer me, how about I check for myself." It wasn't until Mark yanked Tiffany off of the couch and onto the floor that she realized what was about to happen.

Forcefully bunching her skirt above her hips and ripping her pink Barbie panties off, Mark spread Tiffany's legs open with his big thighs and calloused hands. He then bent down and examined her young pussy as if he had obtained a license and certificate from the American Board of Obstetrics and Gynecology.

"What are you doing?" She screamed, only to have it fall on deaf ears. "Mark...Mark...Please stop!"

"Not until I make sure you haven't been out here hoeing around and giving away what belongs to me." He stopped his examination for a second and looked into Tiffany's crying eyes. "Relax baby girl. You know as well as I do that I wouldn't hurt you. You know I like you Tiffany," He shut his eyes and shook his head. "No, that's not true. I actually love you baby girl and just like it's ok to let a boy touch you if you like him, it's ok for me to do what I'm about to do to you because I love you."

Tiffany took the back of her hand and wiped her snot and tear drenched face. "Wha...wha...what are you going to do?"

Mark's face lifted as he smiled at her and looked adoringly into Tiffany's eyes. Turning his body so that he was directly between her thighs, he released the hold he had on her legs and began to undo his pants. After managing to pull his boxers and jeans down to his ankles without getting all the way up, he dropped all his body weight onto Tiffany.

"First I'm going to make sure that you haven't been giving my pussy away, then I'm going to make love to you so good, you won't even let that little nigga Bobby Jones nowhere near what belongs to me."

Tiffany shook her head from side to side as she began to wildly swing her arms and legs around. Shouting at the top of her lungs did nothing for her but make Mark enjoy what he was doing a little more. She balled her small fist up and started to hit Mark all over his face. Instead of trying to control her punches, Mark just laughed and positioned his long, thick dick at her small entrance. Without warning or thinking about his actions, Mark thrust his full length into Tiffany and started to fuck her as if she were a grown woman.

The pain that shot through Tiffany's body when Mark

entered her untouched cave made her cry out like a wounded animal. There was no way in the world that God would let her endure this pain any longer than she had too, but after crying for her mama, her daddy, and damn near anyone else she felt should've been there to protect her, Tiffany's body and mind finally shut down and let Mark have his way with her. Silent tears mixed with Mark's sweat rolled down her face as she stared at the TV screen blocking Mark's loud grunts out of her ear.

Tiffany's mind went to her favorite part of *The Wiz* which happened to be showing on the TV at that moment where Diana Ross had just went to see Glinda the Good Witch and started to sing the song Home.

"*When I think of home, I think of a place, where there's love overflowing...*" Tiffany mouthed as she stared blankly at the TV screen, her small body roughly rocking back and forth. Watching Diana Ross's teary-face mirror her own. Closing her eyes, Tiffany continued to let her favorite song take her to a place like home as Mark continued to degrade her most prized possession.

"*And I've learned that we must look inside our hearts to find* (Grunt)...*A world full of love* (Umm this pussy is so good he cooed into her ear)...*Like yours like mine* (Damn, I'm about to cum baby)....*Like Home...*"

Just as the song ended, Mark released every one of his small demon seeds into Tiffany's womb, not caring about the consequences of nutting in an eleven-year-old child who had been on her menstrual cycle every month for the last year. After kissing her all over her face, then on the lips, Mark pulled himself from Tiffany and walked to the bathroom, leaving her on the living room floor feeling low and disgusted.

Closing her eyes again, Tiffany prayed to God that this was the first and last time Mark violated her body the way he just did, but just like her prayers before, this one request and her cries went unanswered and fell on deaf ears. This vicious ordeal continued for nearly six months, until Tiffany finally broke down and told her grandmother. Mrs. Emily full of anger went and confronted Mark and Camil. Camil begged her mother to let her and her fiancé handle the situation. But Mrs. Emily kept insisting that the police become involved and Mark wasn't going to stick around for that to happen. He gathered a few things and left the house, never to be seen again.

Camil spiraled down after he left, turning up her usage of cocaine and partying just about every night. Her behavior was reckless and at times became violent towards Tiffany. The more family members tried to step in and help, the more Camil pushed away, diving deeper into depression.

"Camil I'm home," Tiffany announced. She had lost all respect for her mother including the honor of referring to her has such. Instead she opted for her first name.

Camil cracked one of her eyes open after hearing Tiffany. "Yeah so what, clean up this damn house and don't take ya ass out of it until its done," Camil commanded without even opening the second eye.

She didn't care about what Tiffany might have had to complete as far as school was concerned. She didn't even think about the fact that Tiffany had been in school all day and probably was a little tired. None of that mattered to Camil. In truth, having the house cleaned, really didn't matter. It was just one of the many ways Camil oppressed Tiffany, hoping that it made her feel unwanted enough to leave. Camil was tired of being responsible for something and someone she never wanted or asked for.

"Dang can you ask Porsha to at least help me?" Tiffany complained. Before Camil could even answer, she was interrupted.

"Porsha not doin shit," a loud voice yelled coming down the stairs. It was Porsha.

"Porsha on her way out the door" she continued.

"Dressed like that," Tiffany mumbled under her breath.

Porsha looked a hot mess and what she had on didn't make a lick of sense. The red skirt over top of some green leggings was just the beginning of her problem.

"You got something smart to say?" She asked, walking up on Tiffany.

Porsha was both taller and heavier then Tiffany which was a little intimidating at times. Today was one of those days Tiffany didn't want any trouble.

"No not at all," Tiffany replied, putting a fake smile on her face and walking towards her room.

But Porsha wasn't done just yet. She reached out and grabbed a fist full of Tiffany's hair and put her in a light weight chokehold. If it wasn't for Camil intervening, it was no telling where it would have went.

"Let the little bitch go before she run and go tell my mom on me and you," Camil spoke in a calm voice. You know we don't need your grandma coming over here, I don't want to hear her mouth. She already be bitching about what you doing with the money coming from your daddy. That check that came in monthly to Porsha, was the only reason Camil let her live there and treated her with some form of dignity. Porsha knowing that Camil was right hesitantly let Tiffany go, but not before mugging the back of her head so hard that Tiffany almost fell to the ground. It took everything in Tiffany for her not to flip out. She probably would have given Porsha a run for her money but instead opted out. The prom was only a couple weeks away and having scars on her face wouldn't look good in her prom pictures.

"Just make sure you clean up this damn house like I told you to," Camil finished, before leaning over and taking a sniff of the coke residue that was on the table.

Tiffany went into her room to take a few minutes, let out a few tears, and get herself cleaned up. Camil didn't know it, but it was no way Tiffany was cleaning up the house today. She had already made plans with Nasir and he would be by to pick her up soon. She couldn't wait until the day came that she would be out this house forever.

CHATIMA WALKED INTO THE EMERGENCY ROOM AT Carolinas Medical Center looking for her husband, and after speaking to the nurse at the front desk she was told where she could find him. When she arrived to the little room he was in, as she was about to cross the threshold, a detective stopped her.

"He's not allowed any visitors right now," the black, stocky detective said, holding his arm out.

Chatima looked around him and could see Hassan sitting on the bed with a bloody patch over his shoulder. She almost began to cry seeing him laid up like that, but the lawyer in her kicked in first. She reached into her bag and pulled out her credentials.

"If he's under arrest, how about you let me know the charges," she asked, passing the detective one of her cards.

The detective looked down at the card then back up at Chatima. He gave her a rundown of the charges, which included 1 a felon in possession of a firearm, 2 Possession of a firearm without a license, 3 Discharging a firearm in public and 4 reckless endangerment.

Chatima looked over the detective's shoulder again, shaking her head at Hassan at what he had gotten himself into.

"Well unless you feel like violating my clients 5th and 6th Amendment rights to counsel, I suggest you step to the side," she warned the detective.

He did the right thing by stepping to the side and letting her in. Chatima made sure she slammed the door behind him so he couldn't hear their conversation.

"What in the hell is going on Hassan?" she quickly asked.

"Nothing much babe, just some fools tried to jack me at the light earlier. I let'em have it tho".

Chatima shook her head, looking down at the hand-cuffs. It was times like this she wished that Hassan wasn't in the game, or at least not as deep as he was. Since Hassan was at the top of the food chain, there was always somebody out there trying to take his place.

"Damn you look sexy as hell when you mad," Hassan joked, while reaching down and grabbing Chatima's ass with his free hand.

Chatima pulled away and couldn't help but to smile, thinking about how crazy her husband was.

"So how does it look?" Hassan asked.

Chatima wasn't the best lawyer in the city but she

wasn't a slouch either. Having her own private practice gave her a lot of flexibility, which in turn allowed her to fight just a little bit harder for her clients. Every district attorney she battled in the courtroom respected her for that and knew that they needed to be on point at all times dealing with her. Most of the times, the D.A. would rather work out some sort of plea with her instead of going through the formalities of going to trial.

"I'm going to make a few calls and see if I can get the charges reduced. In the meantime, how bout you try to stay out of trouble. I don't understand why you have to be so involved still," Chatima voiced before pulling out her phone and stepping out of the room.

She was about to use all of the juice and connections she had for her husband.

CAMIL NODDED BACK OFF FOR A FEW MINUTES, BUT woke back up to see if Tiffany had started cleaning the house. It was dead silent, except for the few kids that were playing outside.

"TIFFANY," Camil yelled out as she looked around the house.

The house looked the same as it did before she had went to sleep. Clothes were still all over the place, along with empty Chinese boxes and other trash. Dirty dishes was still in the sink and the cat's litter box was starting to stink. Camil was mad as hell, even though she and Porsha were the ones who caused the mess.

"TIFFANY," Camil yelled out again while storming up

the stairs towards Tiffany's room. "I thought I told ya ass..."

Camil stopped in mid-sentence, pushing the door open and seeing that Tiffany wasn't there. "TIFFANY," she yelled out again, walking through the rest of the house. No one was home.

Now Camil was really pissed and thought about all the painful ways she wanted to discipline Tiffany when she returned.

"Oh this lil bitch must have lost her fucking mind," Camil mumbled to herself, walking back down the stairs to retrieve her phone.

She tried calling Tiffany but it went straight to voice-mail, only making Camil even more upset. This type of disobedience was not going to be tolerated and Camil planned on dealing with it just as soon as Tiffany walked back through the door. Little did she know, Tiffany didn't have any plans on coming home any time soon.

CHAPTER TWO

Nasir looked over at Tiffany who was laying across his bed, snacking on some Chili Cheese Fritos while watching TV. She was a 10 all the way around the board and Nasir didn't know how much longer he could go without tasting some of her goodies. He and Tiffany hadn't had sex yet and it wasn't because Nasir hadn't pressed the issue. But he figured Tiffany was still a virgin because every time they got close she would freeze up and he wasn't the type to just keep going. Nasir wanted it to be special for Tiffany. He knew she had had a hard life, so if it was patience that she needed he would be just that because he truly loved her. At first, he thought that today might end up being the day but Tiffany's cycle coming on had cancelled all those thoughts.

"You just gonna lay here and eat Fritos all day," Nasir joked, scooting closer to her.

Tiffany rolled onto her back, playfully reached over and put a few of the corn chips into his face.

"Why, you getting tired of me already," she asked teasingly.

"Hell naw. You can stay here as long as you want". Nasir responded while sneaking in a kiss. Although they had never actually had intercourse, Tiffany had blessed him with some head a few times and he was hoping she would today!

However Chatima knocking on the door, had messed that up too.

"What are you kids doing up in here??" She asked when Nasir opened the door.

"Nothing Ma, just watching TV" he quickly answered. Chatima gave him a yeah right "Boy you act like I ain't never been seventeen, and as for you, if they put out an Amber alert for you, ya ass is outta here," Chatima joked but at the same time was serious looking towards Tiffany.

"Ms. D I'm 18," Tiffany laughed. "Besides, my mom don't care about me enough to...

Tiffany got quiet, thinking about the words she was saying about her own mother. Not having the best relationship with her mother growing up, Chatima could feel her pain. She couldn't understand how someone could be so mean to a child who was as beautiful and smart as Tiffany. If Tiffany wasn't so ashamed of who her mother was, Chatima would have reached out and gave her a piece of her mind. Messing around with Tiffany, Chatima knew that it was going to be a long time before Tiffany introduced them.

"So look, I'm about to go and pick ya father up. They gave him a bail this morning, so I'm going to need for you guys to keep an eye on your sister. Chatima told Nasir as she stood by the door. "Oh and that recruiter will be here around 3:00 so don't...

"Mom I already know," Nasir said cutting her off.

The University of Kentucky had a scholarship waiting for him but UNC was also interested in making him a part of the team. Chatima was excited about UNC more than anything and that was because she graduated from there. However at this point, Chatima wasn't about to let anything come in-between Nasir going to college. Tiffany was cute and all, but Chatima wasn't going to let her spoil things for him neither.

Tiffany didn't want to be around when the college recruiter came to the house, so she got up, and called Jayden. They both decided to go shopping for their prom gown. Nasir really wanted her to stay but Tiffany wanted to give him his space for what possibly could have been his life changing moment. She really wished that she was going off to College as well and although she was smart enough. Her home life had derailed her further education dreams for a while. Tiffany rarely had time to complete homework assignments, she was too busy cleaning up the house or trying to stay away long enough to give her mother time to fall asleep. The school work she did do was for Nasir, she felt that he had the best chance at being successful, so she poured all her energy into him.

HASSAN WAS BROUGHT OUT TO THE RECEIVING ROOM and had to sign a few documents in order to get his property. With him already being a convicted felon, his bail was set at 100 thousand. Muwah! Chatima gave him a huge kiss when he walked out into the lobby. His arm was in a sling, but that didn't stop Hassan from wrapping his good arm around her waist. "These muthafuckas took my DNA," Hassan fussed.

"Yea and they better had showed you a warrant for it," Chatima shot back.

A warrant had definitely been issued. Since there had been blood recovered from Hassan's car, after the shootout, it was considered evidence of a crime which made it permissible for them to collect his DNA. Being as though it was an active investigation, Chatima knew that she couldn't contest the warrant.

"So now what?" Hassan asked, looking for some type of direction.

His DNA was crucial and once it was ran through the system, he knew old skeletons were going to start coming out of the closet. One of the more serious crimes he was worried about being connected to was a murder, which had the potential to put him away for the rest of his life.

"Aside from this lingering over ya head, you need to find out who was trying to rob you," Chatima said as they walked over to the car. "If these nigga out here bold enough to try and rob you...

"I don't think they were trying to rob me," Hassan cut in. "If they wanted to rob me, they could have done a better job than that. I think those niggas was trying to kill me."

Hassan had a lot of people in the streets who loved him but he also had his fair share of enemies. One being SK, a guy he had grew up with, who also had the North side of Charlotte on lock. Up until now, it didn't seem like SK would try his hand with Hassan but money, power and respect could always change how any man felt. Hassan definitely wanted to see if SK was behind the attempt and if he was, it was going to be on.

BEFORE TIFFANY WENT TO THE MALL, SHE DECIDED TO stop by her house and grab a few things knowing that her mother and Porsha probably weren't there. It was the first of the month and Porsha had received her monthly check from her father's death. Whenever that money hit the house Camil and Porsha was inseparable. They would party and shop all week until there wasn't a dime left. Tiffany slowly opened the front door, she looked around to make sure her mother or cousin wasn't anywhere in sight. The quietness of the home confirmed to her that she was indeed alone. Quickly she ran into her bedroom and grabbed her book bag and placed the few panties and bras she had into the bag. She didn't have very many outfits except for the ones Nasir had purchased for her on her birthday and Valentine's Day. She really loved him and knew that he loved her as well. As she was heading back out the door she was blocked by Camil and Porsha coming up the walkway. Before she could turn and try to head back in before being seen, Camil was already yelling her name. "Tiffany where in the hell your little ass been?" Tiffany was hoping that she would come inside the house before starting her outburst. It was a bunch of people standing outside and she didn't want to get embarrassed. But Camil didn't care about any of that and continued.

"Bitch I asked you where the fuck have you been?" this

time yelling loud enough for everyone to hear. All eyes turned in their direction.

"Camil can we go into the house please?" Tiffany tried to reason.

"Who the fuck you think you talking too? We go where I say we go, and why the fuck didn't you clean this house up like I told you?"

"Why I got to be the one to clean it up and you and Porsha are the ones that messed it up?"

"I don't care who messed it up, you clean it up because I told you and you live in my house so I don't have to explain shit. Camil barked while standing in front of Tiffany and pointing her finger in her face.

"Camil I don't want to disrespect you, but get your finger out my face."

"Oh Auntie I know she not breaking bad on you" Porsha chimed in.

"You lucky I just got my nails done or I would whoop your little ass out here in front of everybody" Camil exclaimed. Tiffany was so mad but she was trying to contain her hurt and anger.

"Well I don't mind breaking a few nails and fucking her little ass up, just give the word Auntie" Porsha said placing her hand in Tiffany's face.

"Porsha you better leave me da fuck alone".

"Or what? Porsha based, stepping in closer.

Onlookers began to come closer and watched as the confrontation escalated.

"Porsha I'ma tell you one more time," Tiffany warned, balling both of her fist up.

Porsha went to try and push Tiffany and that's when all hell broke loose. Tiffany cocked back and punched Porsha in her face. Porsha countered, and the two exchanged a number of punches. Tiffany had Porsha up against the house, giving her the business. All the anger, all the pain and confusion Tiffany was feeling came out at that very moment. Tiffany kicked and punched Porsha to the ground, and once she was down, Tiffany got on top of her, and began wailing blows to her face. Porsha couldn't do anything, but take the ass whooping Tiffany was handing out.

But then Camil jumped in and grabbed Tiffany by the hair pulling her off Porsha. Tiffany was about to swing on her but caught herself before throwing a punch. Camil was swinging Tiffany's head from side to side, giving Porsha enough time to get up and grab Tiffany and sling her to the ground. The loud thump of Tiffany's head hitting the concrete made everyone cringe. But it didn't stop Porsha, who now stood over top of Tiffany and began kicking her all in her back and stomach. Two police officers that were on foot patrol, saw the ruckus and ran up the street. Tiffany blacked out, just as they were grabbing Porsha up off her.

ABOUT THE AUTHOR

Blake Karrington is an Essence Magazine® #1 Bestselling novelist. More than an author, he's a storyteller who places his readers in action-filled moments. It's in these creative spaces that readers are allowed to get to know his complex characters as if they're really alive.

Most of Blake's titles are centered in the South, in urban settings, that are often overlooked by the mainstream. But through Blake's eyes, readers quickly learn that places like Charlotte, NC can be as gritty as they come. It's in these streets of this oft overlooked world where Blake portrays murderers and thieves alike as believable characters. Without judgment, he weaves humanizing back stories that serve up compelling reasons for why one might choose a life of crime.

Readers of his work, speak of the roller coaster ride of emotions that ensues from feeling anger at empathetic characters who always seem to do the wrong thing at the right time, to keep the story moving forward.

In terms of setting, Blake's stories introduce his readers to spaces they may or may not be used to - streetscapes with unkept, cracked sidewalks where poverty prevails, times are depressed and people are broke and desperate. In Blake storytelling space, morality is so curved that rooting for bad guys to get away with murder can sometimes seem like the right thing for the reader to do - even when it's not.

Readers who connect with Blake find him to be relatable. Likening him to a bad-boy gone good, they see a storyteller who writes as if he's lived in the world's he generously shares, readily conveying his message that humanity is everywhere, especially in the unlikely, mean streets of cities like Charlotte. Blake currently writes for Penguin Random House well as Urban Books.

ALSO BY BLAKE KARRINGTON

Blake Karrington Collection

Made in the USA
Columbia, SC
07 June 2025